GHOST OF THE JEDI

A haunted library . . .

Tash stepped into the light. As her eyes adjusted, she saw a large circular room. The walls were lined with hundreds of shelves, and on the shelves were rows and rows of ancient, dust-covered books. Two antique tables made of carved wood stood in the center of the room, with sturdy wooden chairs beside them.

I found it, she told herself. *I found it!*

In the midst of her own wonder, Tash heard the voice that had awakened her. But this time it did not whisper. It roared around her, loud, harsh, and full of rage.

GET OUT!

Look for a preview of Star Wars: Galaxy of Fear #6, *Army of Terror*, in the back of this book!

titles in Large-Print Editions:

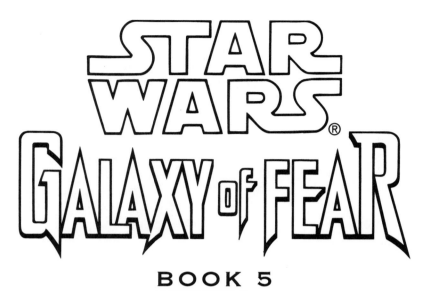

BOOK 5

GHOST OF THE JEDI

JOHN WHITMAN

Gareth Stevens Publishing
MILWAUKEE

To Lucy Autrey Wilson, for giving me the chance

For a free color catalog describing Gareth Stevens' list of high-quality books and multimedia programs, call 1-800-542-2595 (USA) or 1-800-461-9120 (Canada). Gareth Stevens Publishing's Fax: (414) 225-0377.
See our catalog, too, on the World Wide Web: http://gsinc.com

Library of Congress Cataloging-in-Publication Data

Whitman, John.
    Ghost of the jedi / by John Whitman.
       p. cm. — (Star Wars: galaxy of fear)
    Summary: Zak and Tash hope to defeat the evil scientist Gog by finding the lost Jedi library on the abandoned space station Nespis 8, but that storehouse of knowledge is supposedly cursed and guarded by the ghost of a Jedi.
     ISBN 0-8368-2239-0 (lib. bdg.)
     [1. Science fiction.] I. Title. II. Series.
PZ7.W5925Gh   1998
[Fic]—dc21   98-21438

This edition first published in 1998 by
Gareth Stevens Publishing
1555 North RiverCenter Drive, Suite 201
Milwaukee, Wisconsin 53212 USA

Printed in the United States of America

1 2 3 4 5 6 7 8 9 02 01 00 99 98

PROLOGUE

The shuttle's door opened onto the gray landscape of a dead world. The wind howled across the dry plain, whistling among sharp, jagged slabs of rock that seemed to grow out of the ground like stone trees.

Borborygmus Gog stumbled out of the shuttle. He was frustrated.

His frustration turned to pure hatred when he saw who was waiting for him on the planet's surface.

"What an unexpected pleasure," he sneered.

Darth Vader withstood the howling wind, stronger than the jagged rocks around him. "I am here to fix Project Starscream."

Gog glared. "Project Starscream does not need to be fixed."

Vader tilted his head forward, looking down on the doctor. "Are you certain? Hoole has proved himself to be a formidable enemy. I warned you before not to be overconfident. Now Hoole has ruined the first four stages of Starscream, and he is still on the loose, thanks to your incompetence."

The skin on Gog's back rippled. He hated Vader, hated his power and his arrogance. Gog wanted that power—more than anything he wanted to take Vader's place beside the Emperor's throne. Gog was a Shi'ido, a shapechanger. He felt the urge to transform into a wampa ice beast and rip out Vader's throat. He eyed the lightsaber hanging from Vader's belt. He was sure he could reach Vader before the Dark Lord drew his weapon.

But Vader also commanded the Force, and against that, Gog had no defense. At least not yet.

He said, "The project is at a very important stage. The fifth experiment is crucial. Besides, the Emperor himself put me in charge of Project Starscream. It is *my* responsibility."

Vader's breath rasped through his face mask. "And the Emperor himself has asked me to make sure it proceeds with no interference. I have already ordered the deaths of Hoole and his family."

"No!" Gog blurted.

The Dark Lord's voice was threatening. "What?"

Gog recovered himself and said calmly, "That is, there is something peculiar about Hoole's niece and nephew—especially the niece. They are worth further study."

Vader scoffed. "You tried using them with your Nightmare Machine project and failed. Now they threaten everything."

"But—"

"The order is given," Vader interrupted. "I have already sent an assassin to find them."

With that, Vader whirled around and strode away. Somewhere out there, his ship and his soldiers lurked.

Gog resisted the urge to draw his blaster and shoot Vader in the back. The Dark Lord would know without turning around if he even reached for his weapon. Vader had the Force.

The Force. If his plans were to succeed, Gog needed something to defeat the Force.

A cold smile crept across Gog's lips. He had not told Vader why Hoole's niece and nephew—especially the niece—interested him. And why the fifth experiment was so important.

It had to do with the Force.

Gog knew he had to act fast if he was to beat Vader.

He laughed to himself. Vader wanted the Arrandas killed. Gog wanted them alive.

Hoole and his friends would be lucky if Vader's assassin found them first.

CHAPTER

The laser blasts came close. Too close.

One of the energy bolts glanced off the side of the ship, and Tash and Zak felt the *Shroud* buck under the blast. But the shields held. The *Shroud* was a good ship.

"She'll hold together," Zak said. "I think."

As if determined to prove him wrong, another laser bolt struck the ship, sending a shock wave from stem to stern.

"There are two more coming in," Deevee said.

"I see them," Uncle Hoole said tightly.

He banked the ship hard to the left. As the ship spun, Tash caught a glimpse of one of the ships that was chasing them.

An Imperial Star Destroyer.

A dozen laser cannons sent energy beams streaking

toward them. Luckily, the *Shroud* was fast, and Hoole managed to slip away from most of them.

"We can't take another hit like that!" Zak said.

"Quiet," Hoole ordered. "I've almost loaded the coordinates for the hyperspace jump."

Tash tried not to think about the facts. Imperial Star Destroyers were the most powerful ships in the galaxy. They were huge, and had hundreds of weapons that could turn most other ships into space vapor. Despite their size, they were also incredibly fast. Very few ships could outrun them. One Star Destroyer could wipe out a fleet of smaller ships.

And four of them were chasing the *Shroud*.

They had been tailing Hoole and the Arrandas since their recent escape from the Hologram Fun World. For awhile Hoole thought he had lost them, but the Imperial ships had merely sent a signal to another fleet, and now they were nearly surrounded.

A direct hit from a Star Destroyer's cannon made the ship groan. A warning light flashed on the control panel.

"We've lost the main deflector shield!" Zak called out. "The next shot will vaporize us!"

"Almost there," Hoole said to himself. His fingers flew frantically over the controls.

"They're firing again!"

"There!" Hoole said. He pulled a large switch on the *Shroud*'s control panel. The ship lurched forward as though dragged by giant hands, and plunged into the streaking white light of hyperspace.

A few hours later, the *Shroud* still hurtled through the swirling whiteness of hyperspace. In the cockpit, four figures huddled over the control console, their faces lit by the red glow of the instrument panel as the *Shroud* traveled through the most desolate parts of the galaxy.

"Where are we?" asked Tash Arranda.

"I don't recognize any of these star charts," said her brother, Zak.

"If I'm not mistaken," said the droid DV-9, "these coordinates will take us far into the Outer Rim. This is the least colonized part of the galaxy, and the farthest away from the center of Imperial power."

"Correct, Deevee," replied Hoole curtly.

Tash and Zak exchanged glances. For the seven months they had known him, Uncle Hoole had been close-mouthed and stiff-necked. They figured he was constantly in a bad mood because he was a Shi'ido. The Shi'ido species tended to be more serious than humans. But for the past several hours, Hoole had burned with the intensity of a superlaser. He had not left the cockpit once as he piloted the *Shroud* on a frantic star-hopping course, taking them from one star system to another, never stopping, never even slowing down.

Zak pointed to an indicator light that flashed an alarming shade of red. "One of the power couplings is overheating."

"Ignore it," Hoole said.

Zak blinked. He had a mind for mechanics and knew what the warning light meant. "If we don't let the engines cool, the power coupling could blow, and—"

"Ignore it," Hoole snapped again. "That is the least of our concerns."

Tash looked at her brother, who mouthed three words: This. Is. Bad.

Tash wondered how much worse things could get after their escape from the Hologram Fun World. Zak and Tash had nearly been trapped there by an evil scientist named Borborygmus Gog. They had been saved only by their own quick thinking, the help of a good-hearted gambler named Lando Calrissian, and the courage of Uncle Hoole. Like all Shi'ido, Hoole had the power to change his shape. Disguised as an Imperial stormtrooper, he had freed Tash, Zak, and the others, and they had slipped from Gog's clutches. But their escape did not seem to ease Hoole's tension.

"Uncle Hoole," Tash asked gently, "can you tell us any more about what's going on?"

Hoole clenched his jaw as he punched new coordinates into the *Shroud*'s navicomputer. "I know little more than you do, Tash. Gog is working on an experiment called Project Starscream. The Imperial government is involved at the highest levels. Not only have we made ourselves Gog's enemies, we may have fallen under the eye of the Emperor himself."

Tash and Zak both swallowed hard. The *Emperor*? Tales

of his power, and his cruelty, were known throughout the galaxy.

When their adventures had begun, and Hoole had started to act so strangely, Tash at first had thought her uncle was working for the Empire. He always seemed to know what the Imperials were doing and where to find them. But slowly Tash had realized that Hoole wasn't an Imperial. In fact, he seemed to be working *against* the Empire.

A new thought crept into Tash's mind. Was Hoole a Rebel? Perhaps Hoole was spying on Gog for the Rebels. Tash was pretty sure that Hoole knew some Rebels. Once, they all had been rescued from one of Gog's experiments by an odd group of travelers—two men, a woman, two droids, and a Wookiee. At the time, Tash had thought their rescuers were Rebels. She still thought so.

Zak interrupted her thoughts. "If the whole Empire is after us, what are we going to do?"

Tash looked directly at Uncle Hoole and said meaningfully, "Maybe we should try to contact the Rebels."

Hoole said without hesitation, "That might work, Tash, if we knew how to contact them."

"You mean, you don't know how?" she challenged.

Hoole raised an eyebrow. "Of course not. If the Rebels were that easy to find, the Empire would have destroyed them long ago."

"Oh," she said, disappointed. "I just thought . . . I mean . . ."

Hoole almost smiled. "You thought I was a Rebel? No,

Tash, I have no more connection with the Rebel Alliance than you do."

"But . . . then how did you learn about Project Starscream? How do you know so much about Gog, and why does he seem to know you?" Tash said. "Why were you investigating his experiments?"

Hoole paused. "I have my reasons. But you've given me an idea, Tash. Strap yourselves in."

Tash had no time to repeat her question as Hoole punched a new set of commands into the navicomputer. She and Zak slipped into their crash webbing and Deevee braced his mechanical body against the hull of the ship as the *Shroud* groaned into an even higher speed. Gauges bleeped angrily and the engines began to whine. Just when Zak and Tash thought the ship would burst at the seams, Hoole pulled back on a lever and the white streaks of hyperspace gave way to a brilliant starfield. In the distance they could see a bright yellow planet.

"What's that?" Tash asked.

Hoole guided the ship toward the growing yellow sphere. "It is a place far from Imperial eyes. With luck, it's also where we'll find out how to contact the Rebels."

"Thank goodness we've found someplace safe," Deevee sighed.

Hoole turned his dark eyes on the droid and the two young humans. "I did not say we were safe. We are entering a wretched hive of scum and villainy."

The *Shroud* rocketed planetside. It settled almost unnoticed into a fleet of old freighters docked on the outskirts of a small town that baked under the heat of two blazing suns. They climbed from their ship and Hoole led them to a dusty lot, where a tall insectoid creature rented and sold transport vehicles. After some haggling, Hoole rented a creaking landspeeder that barely managed to hover off the ground. The landspeeder's repulsors whined as Zak, Tash, and Deevee clambered aboard.

Moments later, the landspeeder carried them away from the settlement and out into a wide, flat desert.

Tash stared at the horizon, where yellow sand met a clear blue sky. "I think this whole planet is made of sand," she muttered.

"That is correct," Hoole replied. "This place is called Tatooine. I did research here once. It is an dry, unpleasant planet. I was happy to leave it."

"Then what are we doing here?" Zak asked.

"You will see," Hoole answered.

Hoole guided the landspeeder far out into the empty desert. The terrain was so barren and lifeless that Tash thought Hoole had made a mistake. But just when she was convinced that they were lost, a massive fortress appeared on the horizon, squatting like a toad at the foot of a large, rocky mountain.

Hoole pulled the landspeeder up to the gates of the structure and jumped out. As he approached the doors, a large

11

electronic eye popped out of a hatch and scanned him. Then it asked a question in a language neither Zak nor Tash understood.

"I wish to see your master," Hoole replied in Basic, the galaxy's universal language. "Tell him Hoole is here."

The sentry eye retreated through the hatch. A moment later a deep rumble shook the ground, and the great gates opened to admit them. Beyond the gates, a hallway led into darkness like a passage into the underworld.

"Stay close to me," Hoole ordered.

He didn't have to tell them twice. Zak and Tash clung to his blue robe as they followed him down the hallway.

Tash heard a sharp, steady *click-click* sound from the shadows. Turning, she saw a large mechanical spider stalk slowly past them, its metal legs scratching against the floor. A large, transparent globe bulged from its belly. Inside the globe floated a living brain.

"Disgusting," Tash gagged.

"A brain spider," Deevee noted. "Fascinating. I had heard of such things, but I'd never seen one."

"Well, I hope I never see another one," Zak added with a shudder.

A moment later they were halted by two pig-like Gamorrean guards. Once again Hoole stated his name, and the guards let him pass.

Where is he taking us? Tash thought to herself. Then something occurred to her that was more frightening than a brain spider: Uncle Hoole was known in this place.

As they approached the end of a hall, Tash heard the sound of music and voices drifting up from below. And as soon as they started down the wide stairway, Tash's senses were assaulted by the loudest, strongest, most sickening collection of noises, smells, and sights they had ever encountered.

"Oh, my," Deevee gasped.

In a wide audience hall, crowds of aliens laughed, ate, drank, and fought. A gang of Gamorreans wrestled on three low benches and tables. Six multi-legged creatures were playing a dice game in one corner, while in another, an alien band played a frantic tune. The entire chamber was a riot of activity, except for one curious corner where a quiet man sat observing the madness.

In the center of the large room, a space had been cleared where four humans were tormenting a small, rodent-like Ranat. The Ranat had been blindfolded and his ears plugged with wax. The poor creature squealed and stumbled around, completely blind and deaf. The humans dodged away from the Ranat, laughing at their cruel game of tag.

In the middle of this chaos, on a high platform, sat a large, slug-like Hutt, smacking his lips as he stuffed live eels into his mouth with loud slurps. The Hutt laughed as the blind and deaf Ranat fell to his knees.

Hoole descended into the craziness and strode up to the platform. As if on cue, the music stopped, the cruel game of tag ended, and all eyes turned to the newcomers. The massive Hutt let out a deep, rumbling laugh and stared down at the Shi'ido and his companions.

"Well, well!" boomed the creature on the platform. "If it isn't Dr. Hoole himself! I always knew that someday you would fall into my hands once more! Welcome back to the palace of Jabba the Hutt!"

CHAPTER

Jabba the Hutt.

The name boomed through Tash's brain and sent a tremor down her spine.

Jabba the Hutt.

Everyone in the galaxy knew that name. Jabba was legendary. He was a gang boss and a crime lord. Ruler of an underground empire of smugglers, thieves, and assassins. Older kids used his name to scare younger children: ''You'd better watch out or Jabba will come and grab ya.'' Jabba's name was a code word for every danger that lurked in the shadows of the galaxy.

To Tash, Jabba had always been just that, though—a word. She had never thought he was real. Yet now she stood before the mighty Hutt himself, who rolled in his folds of fat.

And Uncle Hoole knows him!

15

Tash looked up at her uncle, a thousand questions threatening to pour out of her mouth. But she bit her lip and held them back. This was no time to interrupt.

"Greetings, Jabba," Hoole said in a clipped voice. "It has been a long time."

"Not long enough," the Hutt rumbled. "Hutts have long memories. I don't forget that you walked out my door years ago."

"I assure you, great Jabba, that it was nothing personal," Hoole replied. "I walked away from many others, including some enemies of yours." Hoole's voice was measured. The Shi'ido did his best to look polite and friendly, but he made sure to meet the intense gaze of the crime lord.

Tash sensed that an important game—maybe even a game of life or death—was being played. If Uncle Hoole offended Jabba, the Hutt might lose his temper and have them killed. But if Hoole showed any sign of weakness, Jabba might lose respect, and have them killed out of sheer boredom.

Jabba reached into a water-filled bowl and pulled out a toad-like creature. It squealed loudly as it struggled to escape Jabba's grasp. The squealing stopped as the massive Hutt dropped the live toad into his mouth. Jabba licked his fingers. "Now then, what brings you to my humble abode?"

Hoole said, "I need your help."

"Ha, ha, ha!" The entire room erupted into laughter, with Jabba's voice booming over the others. Weequays,

Rodians, and a dozen other species chittered and gurgled in amusement.

"I do not understand what is so humorous," Deevee whispered.

"It's like the whole galaxy's laughing at us," Zak muttered.

Hoole glared at his nephew. Then he turned back to Jabba, who said, "And why should I help you? I could just as easily feed you to the marvelous rancor I just acquired."

Hoole swallowed. Zak thought he looked like a gambler about to play his last card. The Shi'ido said, "Because I'm worth more to you alive than dead. Besides, if you help me, you know I'll owe you a favor."

The creatures surrounding the Hutt murmured. Jabba lowered the heavy lids of his bulging eyes and rumbled "Hmm . . ."

Tash looked at Deevee and whispered, "What did he just do?"

Deevee's circuits seemed to be shaking. "Master Hoole has just offered to put himself in Jabba the Hutt's debt. Hutts *always* collect on their debts."

When Jabba finally spoke, his voice was triumphant. "I am inclined to be generous today, Hoole. Especially since you did me the favor of eliminating one of my rivals when you destroyed Smada the Hutt."

Tash blinked. They had encountered Smada the Hutt on D'vouran, the living planet. But they hadn't told anyone. How could Jabba possibly have known?

17

Jabba seemed to read her mind. "Information travels far, and it all ends up here," he said, tapping his chest with one plump finger. "I know you caused Smada's very timely death."

"No, we didn't!" Tash blurted out. Then her throat tightened up as she felt all the eyes in the room turn toward her. "I mean . . . that is . . . he . . . we all needed to work together to get off the planet, but he only thought of himself. He killed himself. Uncle Hoole would never kill anyone."

"Indeed?" Jabba rumbled with amusement. "Are we speaking of the same Hoole that—"

"Great Jabba!" Hoole said quickly. "We would not want to take up more of your time than necessary. Will you give me the information I need?"

The Hutt smiled a slimy smile. "Perhaps, Hoole. Ask your question, and I may do you this favor."

Hoole nodded. "If it is true that all information ends up in your palace, then I want you to tell me how to contact the Rebel Alliance."

Once again Jabba's gang burst into laughter. Hoole stood stone still, but Tash and Zak fidgeted anxiously as Jabba's roaring continued. Finally, the Hutt calmed down. "You amuse me, Hoole. Even *I* do not know where the Rebels are hiding. If I did, I would have sold the information to the Empire long ago, and made a nice profit."

Hoole frowned. "Then you cannot help me, and our bargain is cancelled." He turned to go.

"Wait!" the Hutt boomed. Tash could tell that, despite his arrogance, Jabba wanted to do Hoole a favor. He wanted to have the Shi'ido in his debt. The crime lord continued, "I don't know where the Rebels are, but I have heard stories of strange activities in the Auril system. Rumor has it that the Jedi are somehow involved."

Tash's heart skipped a beat. The Jedi! Ever since she first heard of them, Tash had been fascinated by the Jedi. She had read everything she could about them and their control of the mysterious Force. She had even dreamed of becoming one—but the Jedi were supposed to be extinct, wiped out by the Emperor. Could there still be Jedi Knights left in the galaxy?

Hoole studied the Hutt closely. "There are no Jedi left. Are you seriously suggesting we look for help from the Jedi?"

Jabba raised his fat hands. "I am merely passing along information. Unusual events are taking place in the Auril system, and they are said to have something to do with the Jedi. That is all."

Hoole considered a moment longer, then gave a slight bow. "You have my thanks."

Motioning for Zak, Tash, and Deevee to follow, Hoole turned and left the room. Just as they reached the exit, they heard Jabba's voice thunder after them, "And remember, Hoole, you now owe me a favor!"

The Hutt's laughter seemed to follow them out into the open air.

19

CHAPTER

The rented landspeeder hummed across the sands of the desert planet as Hoole sped back toward their waiting ship.

"The Jedi!" Tash said, unable to contain herself. "Could there really be Jedi out there somewhere? Do you think it's true?"

"No," said Hoole flatly.

"Why not?" Tash challenged.

Hoole kept his eyes on yellow dunes before them as he said to his niece, "Tash, you know as well as I do that the Emperor destroyed the Jedi. There's nothing left of them but the illegal stories you've collected from the HoloNet."

Tash frowned. "But then why would Jabba the Hutt tell you to go there?"

Hoole shrugged. "It is true that Jabba knows a lot about

what happens in the galaxy—that is why I risked this visit. But I find it difficult to believe that he has located Jedi Knights that the Emperor doesn't know about. I doubt we would find anything useful if we followed his advice."

"Then what are we going to do?" Zak asked. "Gog is still out there somewhere." He looked at Tash. "Maybe we should try to get in touch with Forceflow."

Forceflow was a contact Tash had made over the galaxy-wide computer network called the HoloNet. She had never met him, but she had exchanged messages with him many times. He was a mysterious figure who spied on the Empire. When the government erased all information about the Jedi from the HoloNet, Forceflow continued to upload stories and legends of the Jedi Knights for people to read. That was how Tash first learned of the fabled Jedi.

Deevee shook his silver-domed head. "That certainly wouldn't get us very far. We have very little information about this contact. We don't even know where he is located. It sounds too risky to me."

Zak scowled. "It's not any riskier than going to see Jabba the Hutt."

"Zak has a point," Hoole mused, "I don't entirely trust this Forceflow. But he seems to know a great deal about recent events. And we are running out of options." Hoole glanced at his niece. "Perhaps, Tash, it is time we met your friend."

They reached the *Shroud* just as Tatooine's twin suns had

begun to set, turning the yellow sand the color of blood. Several small, brown-robed figures scurried around the base of the ship as if sizing it up.

"Hey, get away from our ship!" Zak yelled.

The dwarfish creatures looked up with surprise in their glowing yellow eyes, then scurried into the shadows.

"What were they?" Tash asked.

"Jawas," Hoole replied. "Scavengers. They're cowards, and usually harmless."

Deevee huffed, "Cowards? They seemed rather bold to me. It is not as though our ship were abandoned."

"They may have thought it was." Hoole punched in the code that opened the ship's hatch. He ushered them all in. "Many who go into Jabba's palace never come out again."

Hoole's comment brought all of Tash's unanswered questions back to mind. How did Uncle Hoole know Jabba the Hutt? Had they worked together in the past? Had Hoole been a criminal? Was he still a criminal? If so, why was he pursuing Gog and Project Starscream?

"Tash?"

Uncle Hoole's voice interrupted her thoughts, and she realized that he had been speaking to her. "Hm? What, Uncle Hoole?"

"I said," the Shi'ido repeated sternly, "do you think you can get in touch with Forceflow over the HoloNet?"

"It's hard to say," Tash replied as she headed for the computer terminal in the ship's lounge. "Sometimes he responds right away, and sometimes it's like he's hiding. I think he has to be careful that the Empire doesn't track his signal.''

Tash dropped into the chair and started punching commands into the computer terminal. She loved exploring the HoloNet. Although she was sitting at a computer terminal inside a small ship, the entire galaxy lay at her fingertips. With the push of a button she could listen to music from the planet Bith or study documents from the archives on Coruscant. Even these days, when the Empire restricted access, the HoloNet was still exciting.

Tash typed in her HoloNet code name at the computer's prompt:

MESSAGE FROM: SEARCHER1

Next she typed in Forceflow's name:

MESSAGE TO: FORCEFLOW

And finally, Tash keyed in her message:

NEED YOUR HELP IMMEDIATELY.

She punched in the code to send the message, then turned to Hoole, Zak, and Deevee, who waited anxiously behind her.

''You might want to sit down,'' she suggested. ''He never responds right a—''

Bleep! Bleep!

A beeping interrupted her as a message appeared on the computer screen.

MESSAGE RECEIVED, SEARCHER. WHAT CAN I DO FOR YOU?

''You were saying?'' Zak laughed.

Tash raised an eyebrow. "That was quick." She turned back to the control panel.

PROJECT STARSCREAM HAS GOTTEN TOO HOT FOR US. WE NEED A SAFE PLACE TO HIDE FROM THE EMPIRE AND WE NEED INFORMATION.

Forceflow responded: YES, I HEARD ABOUT WHAT HAPPENED AT HOLOGRAM FUN WORLD. I WARNED YOU NOT TO GET INVOLVED WITH PROJECT STARSCREAM.

"How does he get his information?" Zak muttered. "He knows as much about us as we do."

"Getting information is his specialty," Tash told her brother.

Tash replied: IT'S TOO LATE FOR THAT. CAN WE MEET WITH YOU?

There was a pause. The computer's screen's cursor blinked rapidly in time with Tash's fluttering heart. She had been in contact with Forceflow for over a year now—since before the Empire had destroyed her homeworld—but she had never asked him his real name, nor where he lived. He had given her volumes of information about the Jedi Knights and their ways, and he'd never asked for anything except privacy. Now she felt like she'd asked for too much.

Finally, a stream of words flashed across the computer screen. AFFIRMATIVE. I THINK IT'S TIME WE MET FACE TO FACE. I'M SENDING YOU MY COORDINATES NOW. I'LL BE WAITING.

A moment later, a line of stellar coordinates appeared on the screen.

Tash sighed. "That's it. We're going to meet Forceflow at last."

Deevee gave an electronic sniff. "I hope that we can trust him."

Zak snorted. "It can't be any worse than Jabba's advice."

Hoole examined the coordinates. "Let's hope you're right, Zak, because they've both given us the exact same advice. These coordinates will take us right to the Auril system."

Like Tatooine, the Auril system was in the deserted Outer Rim sector of the galaxy. Once the *Shroud* blasted out of Tatooine's atmosphere, the trip only took a few hours. But it seemed longer, because Deevee took it upon himself to educate Zak and Tash on the history of that entire quadrant of the galaxy. Even as Uncle Hoole prepared to drop the ship out of hyperspace, Deevee continued talking:

". . . and finally, the Auril system was completely abandoned when the Empire took power," the droid droned on as the hyperdrive engines cut off. "These days, there is nothing for a thousand light-years. No developed planets, no Imperial colonies, not even reports of smugglers in the area. There is absolutely nothing out here."

"Oh yeah?" Zak gasped. "What's that?"

The *Shroud* exited hyperspace and cruised into starspecked realspace—but all the stars had been blotted out. Some huge object filled the view screen—an enormous, shadowy object drifting through the cosmos. The massive object loomed larger as the *Shroud* hurtled toward it.

"Look out!" Tash yelled.

They were on a collision course.

CHAPTER

"We're doomed!" Deevee screeched.

Hoole kept calm. Pulling hard on the ship's controls, he veered left. The *Shroud*'s hull groaned under the strain, and they heard the sound of rivets snapping in the metal walls. Despite Hoole's efforts, for a few moments it looked like Deevee had been right. The ship was too close to the side of the massive structure.

"We're not going to make it!" Deevee moaned, covering his photoreceptors with his silver hands.

The *Shroud* scraped along the side of the barrier; the shriek of metal on metal sent shivers down Tash's spine. But then the starship curved up and away from the dark wall and back into the safety of space.

"Great flying, Uncle Hoole!" Tash cheered.

"Yeah, and a great ship too," Zak said, giving the hull of the *Shroud* a friendly pat.

"Indeed," Hoole agreed. "Now, let's have a look at this object. It looks very old, but it does not appear on any of the star charts."

Hoole turned the ship around and this time he approached the object more slowly.

It was a space station, but not one of the small orbital platforms that circled most planets. This looked like the largest space station ever built. If some brilliant beings had wanted to build an artificial continent, or even a small planet, they could not have done better than this.

By the decayed look of the metal, and the pockmarks left by years of asteroid collisions, the station must have been hundreds, maybe thousands of years old. Different areas of the station seemed to have been designed by different engineers as well. It looked as though it had been added to and expanded over the centuries. The station was a dozen kilometers high and its length was impossible to guess—it stretched on forever in every direction.

And it was absolutely dark. Not a single running light, or landing beacon, or environmental glow panel burned anywhere along its length.

"By the Maker," Deevee said softly. "That is Nespis 8."

"Nespis 8?" Zak asked. "You know this place, Deevee?"

"Only from my extensive historical files," Deevee replied sarcastically. "After all, I was a cultural research droid before I become your caretaker, and I was considered reasonably efficient at my job."

Uncle Hoole seemed unconvinced. "Deevee, I thought Nespis 8 was just a legend. Recheck your memory banks."

"What's Nespis 8?" Tash asked.

The droid paused while his computer brain verified the information. "It is confirmed, Master Hoole. Based on its size, and its apparent age, that is indeed Nespis 8."

"What's Nespis 8?" Tash repeated in exasperation.

Deevee ignored her tone. "According to legend, the Jedi Knights built the space station Nespis 8 as a meeting place for scientists from across the galaxy. The station was devoted to knowledge and learning, and it was considered neutral territory. Even if two planets were involved in a brutal war, their scientists could come to Nespis to do research. As knowledge grew, so did the station, until it was supposed to have grown to the size of a small planet. The legends say that Nespis 8 contained all the knowledge in the galaxy. Including," Deevee added, casting a meaningful look in Tash's direction, "all the wisdom of the Jedi."

"The Jedi," Tash breathed the word as if it were a wish.

"That's correct," the droid affirmed. "It is said that the Jedi maintained a library on Nespis that contained all the writings of their ancient masters. But few dared to look for it. I have heard it said that the halls of Nespis 8 are haunted by the ghost of a Dark Jedi—"

"A *Dark* Jedi?" Zak asked, half-joking. "Now there are dark Jedi too?"

"Dark Jedi," Deevee explained, "were Jedi Knights who served the dark side of the Force. Now please let me finish." The droid paused. "They say Nespis 8 fell to the dark side, and the library was put under a curse forbidding anyone to enter. Only a true Jedi could enter the library and resist the dark-side curse. Of course, all of this is just a legend, and not a very convincing one, in my opinion."

"Whooo!" Zak gave a mock shudder. "Dark Jedi curses—scary stuff."

Hoole dismissed the story with a shrug. "The galaxy is full of rumors. This one is nothing more than an old spacer's story"

"Even if it's not," Zak said, "it shouldn't bother Tash. Since she's our resident Jedi, she should be safe as a Wookiee in a tree!"

"Shut up, Zak!" Tash snapped. She hadn't meant to react so sharply, but she didn't like Zak joking about her interest in the Jedi. Sometimes she felt strange sensations, almost like warnings—warnings she hoped were the beginning of the Force growing in her. But her dreams of becoming a Jedi Knight had seemed to fall apart recently. On their last adventure, Tash had had the chance to wield a Jedi lightsaber. She had failed miserably. "Besides," Tash grumbled finally, "everyone knows there's no such thing as ghosts."

"Enough," Hoole said. "We have far more urgent concerns. This is where Forceflow told us to meet him, but this station is enormous. I have no idea where we might find—"

The Shi'ido was interrupted by the bleep of an indicator light.

Zak checked the reading, then pointed toward a wide opening in the side of the space station. "Someone just activated a homing beacon. It's coming from that landing bay."

Hoole looked sidelong at his niece. "Well, Tash, it appears your friend Forceflow is extending his hand to welcome us."

The *Shroud* banked toward the darkened landing bay and settled into a cavernous chamber. To everyone's surprise, as soon as the ship came to a halt, an energy field activated at the edge of the landing bay, blocking out the freezing cold of space. Seconds later, breathable air began to flood the space dock.

"Someone is definitely expecting us," Zak muttered.

"Of course," Tash said. "Forceflow wouldn't let us down."

"Opening the hatch," Hoole declared.

The *Shroud*'s hatch opened with a loud squeal that reverberated through the docking bay. Only the dim glow of the ship's landing lights cut through the darkness. As Tash passed in front of one of those lights, she cast a long, thin shadow that stretched out for thirty meters across the floor.

Her footsteps echoed mournfully. She stopped. As the echoes died, she thought she heard something else. It sounded like cloth brushing against skin, or a soft breath . . .

"Hello?" she called out.

"Hello? Hello? Hello?" the walls of the empty space station replied.

"Creepy," Zak whispered. "It doesn't look like there's anyone here."

"I suppose the systems could have been automated," Deevee suggested.

Zak looked at his sister, who was staring off into the darkness. "Tash, do you sense anything?"

She shrugged. "I don't know. It doesn't matter. I'm not a Jedi, anyway."

Uncle Hoole considered. "Perhaps we should have a look around. Stay close . . ."

Tash wasn't listening. Despite what she had said, she *did* feel something. She just couldn't tell what. In the past, when she sensed danger, it was like a pit opening in her stomach. But this was . . . different. It was like someone was out there, in the darkness, staring at her. She felt like the Ranat in Jabba the Hutt's palace—blind and deaf, trying to touch someone she couldn't see or hear. Before she knew it, she had wandered away from the others, deep into the darkness of the space station. The ship's lights were now only a distant gray blur, almost lost in the thick blackness. Tash waved her hand before her face, but couldn't see it.

She still felt someone's presence.

She groped blindly forward, afraid of stumbling over anything in the dark. She was sure at any moment that she would find something. Something was there, she was sure.

Her hand touched cold metal. She had reached the wall of the docking bay. She felt around for a moment—nothing there. It was just a wall. Confused and frustrated, Tash turned to head back to the others.

As she did, she felt a cold breath on her back, and a heavy hand fell on her shoulder.

CHAPTER

The grip on Tash's shoulder tightened and she let out a yelp of surprise. Her cry bounced back and forth on the walls until it sounded like an army of frightened voices.

"Be silent," said a deep voice. The strong hand on her shoulder turned her around slowly. There was a soft click, and a small glow rod ignited and slowly grew in power, illuminating the air around it. Tash winced, expecting to see someone—or something—horrible.

Instead, she found herself looking up at the most handsome man she had ever seen. His hair was as dark as a midnight sky. His blue eyes twinkled as brightly as stars. His face was creased as if from years of care, and softened only by a dark moustache. He carried himself confidently. He reminded Tash of the gambler Lando Calrissian, but he lacked the roguish air of a con man.

"I will not hurt you," said the man. His voice was smooth and comforting. "You are Searcher1?" he asked, using Tash's HoloNet code name.

"Y-Yes," she managed to say. "You can call me Tash."

The man nodded. "Greetings, Tash. I am Forceflow."

"Forceflow," she repeated, hardly believing it. She had met him at last. The man who had first introduced her to the legends of the Jedi Knights. The man who risked his life to make others aware of the evil acts of the Empire. He looked exactly as she had imagined.

"I did not mean to frighten you," he said.

"You didn't— I mean, I just thought there was nothing behind me but a wall. And then I felt this cold breath, and . . ."

Forceflow pointed his small glow rod toward the wall. A small door had slid open, revealing a passageway beyond. "I came through there. You must have felt the air shift."

His words were drowned out by the clanging echoes of approaching footsteps. Hoole, Zak, and Deevee had heard Tash cry out. A beam of light swept across the wall and settled on them both.

"Tash, are you all right?" Hoole demanded.

Tash blinked in the bright light. "I'm fine, Uncle Hoole."

By this time she had regained her composure. She introduced the others to Forceflow, who shook Hoole's and Zak's hands. He even gave Deevee a slight bow.

"And what should we call you?" Hoole asked. "Forceflow is only your HoloNet code name, isn't it?"

The man hesitated. "Forceflow will do. Now, if you'll follow me, I can take you to a comfortable place, where we can talk."

They waited while Deevee secured the ship in dry dock, then they all followed Forceflow down the passageway he had opened. The corridor led to several intersections, all of them dark. But Forceflow seemed to know his way, lighting their path with his glow rod.

"Pardon me, sir," Deevee asked as they walked. "But am I right in assuming that this, in fact, is Nespis 8?"

Forceflow glanced over his shoulder. "It is. Unless you believe the fools who say Nespis is only a legend."

Hoole said, "But it is hard to believe that such a large and famous space station could remain undiscovered for so long."

Forceflow shook his head. "Nespis is not 'undiscovered.' I have known about it for years. Scavengers and looters come by every now and then to pick over the ruins. And lately, there have been fortune hunters. We'll probably run into a few of them here. Don't worry, they're mostly bored professors who have retired from teaching to try something more exciting."

"Fortune hunters?" Zak asked excitedly.

Forceflow nodded. "Nespis is full of undiscovered treasures—valuable gems, cargo holds filled with spice, things

36

like that. Treasure hunters come looking for anything valuable.''

Hoole had been studying Forceflow closely. Now he asked, ''Why did you want us to meet you here?''

Forceflow answered without hesitation. ''Tash said you were on the run from the Empire.'' Forceflow opened his arms. ''Look around. This is as far from the Empire as you'll get. The life support systems still function on most areas of the station, and you can even run equipment if you find a live power cable. This is where I hide out from the Empire when things get too dangerous.''

''Is that why you sometimes take so long to answer my HoloNet messages?'' Tash asked.

Forceflow nodded. ''Besides, there's something here that may help you defeat your enemies, if you can find it.''

''What?'' Tash asked.

Forceflow turned and looked her right in the eye. ''The Jedi library.''

''You mean it really exists?'' she asked. ''I thought it was just a legend.''

''It *is* a legend,'' Hoole said firmly.

Forceflow shrugged. ''Nespis is supposed to be a legend too, but you're walking in it right now.''

Hoole frowned. ''But the Emperor and Darth Vader hunted down all the Jedi and destroyed any mention of them. It is hardly likely that they would have left behind such a valuable thing as a Jedi library.''

"Unless they couldn't find it," Forceflow responded as he made one final turn and entered a wide chamber. "They say it's very well hidden."

"Who says?" Zak asked.

"They do."

He pointed into the chamber. Like the rest of Nespis, the chamber was cast in deep darkness, but unlike the docking bay, this darkness was softened by the dim light of a half dozen glow panels. At one time, the room must have been a large cargo hold, but now it served as the base camp for a small group of interstellar travelers. There were five or six of these little camps, each separated from the others, and each containing the equipment and supplies of one or two fortune seekers. High above, the ceiling had been replaced by a wide bubble of transparasteel. Beyond it, a bright field of stars twinkled, creating a breathtaking scene that equalled the view of any planet's night sky.

"This place is called the solarium," Forceflow explained. "From here, you can take passageways to almost any part of Nespis 8. Also, what little power is left in Nespis runs through cables in this room. That's why most of the fortune hunters make their camps here."

"Are they friendly?" Tash asked as they approached the fortune hunters' camp.

"Hey, loves!" called out a gray-haired human woman cheerfully, as if answering Tash's question. "Newcomers! Welcome to Nespis 8. What are your names? Where are you from? Say, any chance you passed through Corellia?

That's where I'm from. Name's Domisari of Corellia, but I haven't been back there in months. Haven't even had any news in weeks, and I'd love to hear what's zipping about in the old space lanes. You know what it's like on the treasure trail, never a moment to stop and stare at the stars. So, have you been there?''

Tash and the others just stared at her blankly, not knowing which of her questions to answer first. Domisari burst out laughing. ''Can't keep up with old Domisari, eh?'' She winked. ''Don't worry, no one can.''

''Um, have you been here long?'' Tash asked.

''No, no, dears,'' Domisari laughed. ''Only just arrived. I was hunting fire crystals in the No-ad system before this. But I got tired of the heat there, and thought I'd try my hand at hunting up a few antiquities here. Well, anyway, welcome, welcome!'' Still chuckling to herself, Domisari wandered back among the piles of storage containers, scanning equipment, and food bins that made up her small camp.

Forceflow introduced them to a few other fortune hunters. Unlike Domisari, these had been on Nespis for weeks, and even months. They seemed friendly enough, until Zak asked one of them the wrong question.

''So can you tell us how to get to the Jedi library?''

A grizzled, gray-bearded treasure hunter squinted at him. ''We don't ask questions like that, lad. My hunt is my hunt, and I don't give clues. If you want to be the one to find the library, go out and look for it yourself.'' His eyes glittered mischievously. "But do you think you've got the stomach for the search, lad?"

The warning in the old man's voice put Tash on edge. "What do you mean?"

The graybeard cackled. "You mean to tell me you've not heard of the curse? The library's a forbidden place. Meant only for the Jedi, they say. Anyone else who takes a single book, a single leaf of a book, a single word off a page of a single book, is doomed!"

"Really, sir," Deevee stepped in, "I must insist that you not try to frighten my charges."

"It's not me that'll put a fright in 'em," the treasure hunter replied. "It's the truth. Others have come to look for the library, and some say that it's been found. But no one who found the library ever lived to tell of it. For they're all, every last one of 'em, dead."

Tash and Zak both swallowed nervously, but Hoole cast a cold eye at the old man. "If it's so dangerous, why are you here?"

The graybeard cackled again. "That's the spirit! Don't let an old man scare you. There's a fortune to be made here, if you can survive the curse. But I'll tell you this. I'm the closest of this bunch. I'll find the library." He turned away, chuckling to himself.

Zak whistled. "I'd say that guy's a few coordinates off the space lane."

"Don't mind him," Forceflow said. "These treasure

hunters are kind enough, but they're all in competition to find anything valuable on Nespis, especially the library.''

. ''They don't seem that friendly.'' Zak pointed to another small camp. ''Look at that guy.''

The camper sat in the midst of his supplies. His body was as thin as a blade, and his face was very long, but his cheeks puffed out and were slightly red. He seemed to be contemplating something private. Then, as if feeling Zak's eyes on him, the man turned his head and looked at them. Tash shuddered. He looked at them as though he was looking at his dinner.

Zak wrinkled his brow. ''He looks familiar.''

''A newcomer,'' Forceflow said. ''Like Domisari, he arrived only recently. Come along. I've set up my equipment in a small room right down this hallway.''

As Forceflow guided them down a side passage at the far end of the solarium, Deevee moved up to his side, slipping between him and Tash to ask questions about the history of Nespis 8.

Tash didn't mind. In fact, her feet dragged, and she soon dropped back behind her brother and Uncle Hoole on the way to Forceflow's quarters. Her whole body felt heavy, as though someone were tugging on her jacket to hold her back.

What's wrong with you? she scolded herself. *You should be thrilled. You've been wanting to meet Forceflow for months. Now not only have you met him, but he may help you find a secret Jedi library! Snap out of it, Tash.*

Lost in thought, she almost didn't notice when someone tapped her on the shoulder. The tap came again, harder, and Tash turned to see who wanted her attention.

But no one was there.

CHAPTER

Tash blinked.

The passageway was dark.

"Who's there?" she whispered.

The only response was a gentle shift in the air. A cold breeze passed through Tash. She felt it deep in her bones and shivered.

"Who's there?" she whispered again, urgently.

She thought she heard a long, low, mournful moan, but there was no one in the hallway. Zak and the others had followed Forceflow farther down the passage. She was alone.

Or was she?

"Zak!" she shouted. "Uncle Hoole!"

She ran after them and caught up to them as they turned back in alarm.

"Tash, what's wrong?" the Shi'ido asked.

"Someone tapped me on the shoulder back there," she replied. As she said the words she realized how silly they sounded.

"That's pretty terrifying, Tash," Zak laughed.

"No, I mean, it was someone who wasn't there. I mean . . . I don't know," she stopped. Her heart was pounding. "I felt someone touch me . . . then it was almost as if they walked right through me." She shuddered. "But I didn't see anyone."

Forceflow smiled at her. "Perhaps I can explain. Nespis 8 is a very large station, with hundreds of rooms and hallways. It's so big that it actually has its own weather patterns, like a planet. Some of the rooms have even flooded and become shallow lakes. We get different temperatures, different air currents. Sometimes it feels like someone is breathing down your neck."

"Are you saying what I felt was the *wind*?" Tash asked in surprise.

"Exactly," the man replied.

They reached Forceflow's quarters—a square room that once must have been a research laboratory. Forceflow had filled it with computer equipment. Wires and circuit boards were everywhere. "As you can see I haven't had time to set things up properly. I wanted to bring my computer equipment along this time because it's possible we'll be staying for quite a while. Our search could go on for days or weeks."

"Our search?" Hoole asked suspiciously. "Our search for what?"

Forceflow looked surprised. "Why, the Jedi library, of course."

Hoole furrowed his brow. "Sir, we appreciate your help, but we have some difficulties to deal with. We have no time to chase rumors and legends."

Forceflow paused a moment, then set his clear blue eyes on Tash. "As Tash can tell you, I specialize in gathering information, so I know all about your troubles. I know that you've discovered this mysterious Project Starscream, and that an evil scientist named Gog is after you. But, believe me, you won't be able to save yourselves or stop Project Starscream without help. And the only thing that can help you now is the vast knowledge contained in the Jedi library."

Forceflow turned to Hoole. "If half the stories I've heard are true, the library contains information on Jedi teachings that could help you stop Project Starscream, and maybe even rid the galaxy of the Empire forever."

"What about the curse?" Tash asked. "I mean, if all the other parts of the legend are true, what about the part that says Nespis 8 fell to the dark side, and that a Dark Jedi placed a curse on it?"

Forceflow waived his hand dismissively. "Bantha fodder. Nespis 8 is real, the library is real. The rest is all rubbish."

Hoole touched the long fingers of one hand to his chin as he considered. At last he said, "I am not convinced. But I do agree that this seems to be a good place to hide from the Empire. And I see no reason not to search for this mythical library—as long as it poses no danger for Zak and Tash.''

Forceflow smiled. ''I can assure you there is nothing to worry about.''

Soon afterward, Hoole excused himself to check on the *Shroud*. Zak, who never missed a chance to work on a starship engine, followed, leaving Deevee behind to watch over Tash. The droid and the girl talked with Forceflow for a while, but he seemed even more secretive in person than he had been over the HoloNet. Tash guessed that Forceflow was reluctant to talk in front of anyone he didn't know well. But she was dying to talk to him alone and get to know him better. She turned to her droid companion.

''Deevee, why don't you go back to the *Shroud* and do some research on Nespis 8? It might help us find this Jedi library.''

Deevee tilted his silver head. ''Tash, I can assure you I have all the information I need stored in my memory banks. My computer brain is quite—''

''I know,'' she interrupted, ''but I think it might be useful to do a little *digging*.''

Deevee hesitated, giving the electronic version of a confused blink. But his caretaker program detected no danger. After all, Forceflow was the person they had come all this way to meet. So the droid said, ''Very well,'' and shuffled away.

Tash turned back to Forceflow. At last she had a chance

to speak to her hero. She tried to find the courage to speak her mind. "I just wanted to tell you it's a pleasure, I mean . . . it's an honor to finally meet you."

Forceflow bowed his head modestly. "I wouldn't call it an honor, Tash. We're all in this fight together."

"But you," she searched for the right words, "you're doing so much. The Emperor nearly wiped the Jedi clean out of history. There must be thousands of others like me, who never would have heard of the Jedi Knights if not for you."

Forceflow's eyes twinkled at her. "You would have found out, Tash. Somehow, you would have known. I can tell that about you."

Tash felt herself blush. "How have you managed to keep defying the Empire for so long without getting caught?"

"Just lucky, I guess."

"But you'd have to be a genius to stay one step ahead of the entire Empire. Unless . . ." she hesitated. "Unless you're working with the Rebels."

Now it was Forceflow's turn to hesitate. He shifted uncomfortably, then cast her a sly look. "Remember, *you* said that, not me."

Tash grinned.

"But I'm not important, Tash," Forceflow said sincerely. "You are. From what I know, you and your friends have stumbled onto something very dangerous. This Project Starscream is very top secret stuff. Even I hardly know anything about it, and I've tapped into some high-level information. How did you find out about it?''

Tash began to explain. As she talked, Forceflow listened with such an open, honest look on his face that she found herself pouring her heart out to him. She told him how the Empire had destroyed their home planet of Alderaan, and how she and Zak had been adopted by Uncle Hoole. Forceflow seemed particularly interested in why Hoole had taken them on their first mission to the living planet of D'vouran.

''How did he know?'' the man asked.

''I don't know,'' Tash replied. ''Back then we didn't know anything was going on. But . . .'' She looked around, as though someone might be listening. She felt terrible for what she was about to say, but she had to tell someone, and Forceflow was her only confidante. ''To tell you the truth, I think there's something mysterious about Uncle Hoole. I mean, he's saved us several times, and I know for sure he's not working with the Empire, but the more I learn about him, the more suspicious I get.''

Forceflow raised an eyebrow. ''Like what?''

Tash lowered her voice. ''On D'vouran, we met a crime lord who knew Uncle Hoole. Then a bounty hunter named Boba Fett seemed to know about him too. Even Jabba the Hutt knows him!''

''Well, that's no evidence of anything,'' Forceflow said softly.

''There's more. Recently, my brother and I got ahold of

Hoole's computer files. There are four years missing from his records. No one knows where he was or what he was doing.''

"That is unusual.'' Forceflow paused. "Maybe it's a good idea to keep an eye on him after all.''

Tash shrugged. "I just wish we'd never gotten ourselves caught up in this Project Starscream mess. I wish we were out of it.''

"You will be,'' Forceflow promised. "Just find that library, and I predict you won't have to worry about a thing.''

Tash looked around at the computer equipment piled in Forceflow's room. "Where do you get your information? You seem to know as much about Project Starscream as we do.''

Forceflow suddenly yawned. "Forgive me. I haven't stopped moving since I arrived here, and I still need to finish setting up my equipment. Perhaps we could finish our discussion later?''

Before Tash could answer, he turned to his machines and began to sort through a thick tangle of computer wire.

Dismissed, Tash left Forceflow's small chamber and wandered out into the solarium. Zak and Deevee were just returning from the *Shroud*.

"So you finally dragged yourself away from Forceflow,'' Zak teased. "What do you think of him?''

Tash shrugged. "He's a lot like I imagined. Mysterious, full of secrets . . .'' Her voice trailed off.

Zak laughed. "Looks like Tash has a crush!"

"I do not!"

"Yeah, then why are you turning red?"

Tash felt her cheeks burning. She changed the subject. "What do *you* think of him?"

Zak shook his head. "He's all right, I guess. I mean, this place is more like a floating tomb than a hideout, but it's still better than being at Jabba the Hutt's place." Zak's eyes lit up. "Jabba the Hutt. That's it!"

"That's what?" Tash asked.

"That's where I know that fortune hunter from. I saw him at Jabba's palace!"

Tash was stunned. "That's impossible!"

"No, it isn't," Zak argued. "He could have followed us."

"I'm afraid Tash is right," Deevee said. "That man obviously arrived before we did. How could he have followed us if he was here ahead of us?"

Zak scowled. "There's only one way to find out," he muttered, and started to walk off.

"Zak, where are you going?" Tash hissed.

Deevee sputtered, "Zak I insist that you . . ."

But Zak was already on his way to the thin man's camp.

Tash caught up with Zak and followed him the rest of the way. The man was exactly as they had left him, sitting serenely amid his stacks of supplies, his face settled into the hint of a sneer. He looked at them as they approached, but did not greet them.

"Excuse me," Zak said politely, "but I was just telling my sister that you look familiar. Have we ever met?"

The thin man pursed his lips. "No."

"Oh." Zak tapped his forehead, pretending to search for some old memory. "Are you sure? Maybe on a different planet? Somewhere like . . . Tatooine?"

Silence.

Zak started to fidget under the man's steady glare. Tash jumped in. "Um, okay, maybe not. Sorry to bother you. My name's Tash, Tash Arranda. This is my brother, Zak."

Silence. Then the man's thin lips parted and he spoke two words. "Dannik Jerriko."

"Great. Thanks. Nice to meet you," Tash said, turning away. She could feel Dannik Jerriko's eyes boring into her like laser beams. "Nice going, rancor brain!" she hissed at her brother as they retreated to the other end of the solarium.

"That's him!" Zak whispered back. "He followed us here."

"You're crazy," she insisted. "But even if you're not, so what? If Jabba the Hutt wanted to kill us or Uncle Hoole, he would have done it when we were in his palace. Dannik Jerriko is no threat to us."

Tash said the words with a confidence she didn't really feel. All of her instincts told her that whoever he was, Dannik Jerriko meant them no harm. But she wasn't sure she could trust her instincts anymore. After all, she'd learned the hard way that she wasn't a Jedi and never would be.

Zak shook his head. "Tash, I'm telling you I saw him as clearly as I see him right—" Zak stopped in mid-sentence. He had pointed back toward the thin man's camp, but Dannik Jerriko wasn't there. Zak and Tash stood there in silence, wondering where he had gone.

Then Tash heard Zak mumble something in her ear. "What did you say?" she asked.

Zak looked at her. "I didn't say anything."

Tash furrowed her brow. "Yes, you did. You just mumbled."

Zak rolled his eyes and looked at their droid companion. "Deevee, did you hear me say anything?"

"Not a word," the droid confirmed, "and my auditory sensors are quite well-tuned if I do say so myself."

"Tash, you're getting jumpy," her brother warned. "You're letting this creepy place get to you. Relax. We're hidden from the Empire, and Forceflow is going to help us. What could possibly go wrong?"

At that moment, a triumphant shout echoed through the halls of Nespis 8. "I found it! I found it! It's mine!" someone roared. The treasure hunters in the solarium looked up, startled. The happy cry bounced off the walls so many times and so loudly that Tash had to cover her ears. Joyful laughter followed, then there was brief moment of silence.

Then the walls began to scream.

CHAPTER

Tash threw herself on the ground and covered her ears with her hands. The scream seemed to come from all around her. As it finally faded, she realized that what she had heard were the echoes of some terrible cry.

Beside her, Zak had fallen to the ground too. As he struggled to his feet, he whispered, ''Wh-What was that?''

The old woman, Domisari, was already out of her little camp and running for one of the many passageways leading from the solarium. ''It came from down here!''

By the time Zak, Tash, and Deevee had caught up with her, all the other treasure hunters had joined them, along with Forceflow and Uncle Hoole. Only Dannik Jerriko was missing. The passageway narrowed, and soon they were hurrying single file down a gangway that zigzagged into the bowels of the space station.

"Are you sure it came from here?" Tash whispered to Domisari. "How could you tell with all those echoes?"

"Good ears," was all the old woman said in reply.

The passageway quickly grew cold. Several of the treasure hunters ignited small glow rods, but it stayed chilly.

"Has anyone ever been down here before?" Forceflow asked.

All the treasure hunters shook their heads. One said, "Naw, this was Mangol's territory. None of us wanted to come down here. Too cold."

The farther they got from the solarium, the colder it became. Before long, Tash could see her breath in the dim light of the glow rods.

"Watch it!" someone yelled.

A chasm opened before them, its smooth walls broken only by a steep, almost ladderlike stairway.

"Ventilator shaft," Forceflow guessed. "That's why it's so cold here. Watch your step. That shaft could be two kilometers deep. There's no sign of a bottom."

One by one, the group descended the stairs. Forceflow went first, followed by Domisari and the other treasure hunters. Zak followed, then Tash. Uncle Hoole and Deevee brought up the rear. Tash waited her turn and then slowly walked down, clutching the cold railing, listening as each step made a dull clank on the metal.

The stairs ended at an opening in the wall. Gratefully, Tash stepped away from the chasm on the other side of the stairs and toward the light of waiting glow rods. Forceflow and the other treasure hunters had gathered around something lying on the floor.

"What is it?" Tash asked.

One of the treasure hunters pointed down and said, "Mangol."

The dim light spilled down onto a body. It was the grizzled treasure hunter Zak and Tash had spoken to. He was lying on his back, his face twisted into a mask of horror. His right hand clutched his chest. In his left he held something Tash had only seen in museums. It was a small rectangular object made up of thin leaves bound inside a leather cover.

"What is it?" Zak asked.

"A book," she breathed. "An actual book."

Deevee piped in. "It must be ancient. There has not been a book made in the galaxy in a thousand years."

All writing was done on computers and the texts were stored on data disks. It was far more convenient, but data disks weren't nearly as nice to look at as this antique.

"Do you know what this means?" Forceflow said excitedly. He caught Tash's eye. "It means Mangol must have found the Jedi library. It must be around here somewhere!"

Hoole grimaced. "That's not important right now. How did he die? What happened?"

Deevee knelt down and examined the body carefully. "There is no evidence of a blaster bolt, or a puncture wound. There are no bite marks. He looks too healthy to have been ill."

"Look at his face," Domisari said. "Something scared him before he died."

Suddenly, Tash grew pale. She remembered the cold feeling of someone touching her, the voice whispering in her ears. If the man had found the Jedi library, she thought she knew why he was dead.

"The curse," she said softly. "It's the dark-side curse placed on the library. That must have killed him."

Forceflow snorted. "A curse! Utter nonsense."

"Then what did kill him?" Domisari asked.

At that moment another figure drifted into the pool of light. "What has happened?"

Startled, the whole group turned to find Dannik Jerriko staring back at them.

"Someone was just killed," Hoole stated.

Zak's eyes narrowed. "Where were *you*?" he asked.

Dannik blinked. "I was . . . otherwise occupied. How did he die?"

"We don't know," Hoole answered. "There are no marks of any kind. Deevee, do you have any information on something like this stored in your memory banks?"

The droid paused a moment, summoning up the contents of his computer brain. "Yes, Master Hoole. There are many accounts of mysterious deaths such as this. In each case, the report lists no known cause of death. However . . ." Deevee paused.

"Yes?" Hoole demanded.

". . . many of the reports suggest that the cause of death is the Anzati."

"The Anzati," one of the treasure hunters repeated with a shudder.

The Anzati, Tash thought. They were myths. Legends. No one knew what the Anzati looked like; no one had ever seen one and lived. No one was even sure they existed. But everyone agreed that if they did exist, they were the most terrifying creatures in the galaxy. They were assassins. The Anzati killed but left no mark. Their victims simply died. No one could stop them. No one could escape them.

"Could there be an Anzati on Nespis 8?" Zak asked.

Instead of answering him, Hoole turned to the veteran treasure hunters. "Has anything like this happened before?"

One shook his head. "Not like this. People have disappeared, but Nespis 8 is a huge space station with lots of pitfalls. We always figured that someone just took a wrong step."

Could it have been an Anzati? Tash thought. But even as she did, a chill passed through her, as though someone had touched an ice cube to the back of her neck. Again, she heard a faint whisper in her ear.

No, she thought. *It's not an Anzati. It's not a living thing. It's the curse of the library.*

Forceflow pointed at the book on the floor. "Well, he's dead and nothing can change that. But look at the book. He must have found the library. It must be around here some-where!''

Hoole reached down and pried the book from Mangol's stiff fingers. But the minute he did, the ancient book disintegrated into dust that trickled from Hoole's open hand.

''Curious,'' the Shi'ido mused.

''The book must have been extremely old,'' Forceflow guessed. He looked around. ''We should search for the library immediately.''

Hoole stood up. ''I think not. If there is an Anzati around here, we have no way to protect ourselves. I suggest we all return to the solarium for now.''

Forceflow seemed to bristle. Some of the warmth faded from his eyes. ''You are not in charge here.''

Hoole raised an eyebrow. ''Neither are you. I simply suggest we put safety first.''

The others agreed, over Forceflow's objections. Everyone was eager to find the library, but they had all been disturbed by the mention of the mysterious Anzati. If such a creature did exist, no one wanted to be its next victim.

Carefully, they carried Mangol's body back up the narrow stairs to the solarium. They laid his body in his camp and covered it with a spare sheet. Hoole insisted that Tash, Zak, and Deevee return to the safety of the *Shroud* until they knew just how dangerous Nespis was.

By the time she reached her own small cabin, Tash was exhausted. After fleeing the Star Destroyers, visiting Jabba's palace, meeting Forceflow, and now this—she felt like a great weight was pressing down on her. But she couldn't sleep. She was grateful when her door slid open and Zak slipped into her room.

"Are you thinking about what happened?" he asked.

"What else?" she replied.

Zak shook his head. "I think that Dannik Jerriko has something to do with the treasure hunter's death."

Tash sighed. "Okay, Zak. Suppose you're right and Dannik did somehow follow us to Nespis 8, but managed to get here before us. Why would he kill a harmless treasure hunter?"

"I don't know," her brother retorted. "But he was missing when Mangol died. Remember how he showed up so long after we found the body? Maybe he needed time to circle around so it looked like he'd been behind us all the time."

Tash could only sigh. "I don't know Zak. I don't think it's . . ." She hesitated.

"What?"

"I think it has something to do with the library."

"Do your *feelings* tell you that?" Zak asked.

"I told you, I don't trust that anymore," she said wearily. "I don't know what those feelings mean."

Zak's eyes softened. In the past, he had made fun of Tash and her interest in the Jedi. Now he felt a twinge of guilt. "Tash, you shouldn't say that. Your feelings have been right before. Remember on D'vouran? You knew something was wrong there."

59

Tash nodded. "I know, Zak. For a while, I thought I might be—or could be—a Jedi. But now I think that was just a fluke. When we were on Hologram Fun World, I didn't know what was happening even though we were in danger. Now I just feel like I'm going crazy. That's the opposite of what a Jedi is."

Zak shrugged. "Don't worry about it, Tash. This place is gloomy enough to get on a Jedi Master's nerves. Besides, we don't need the Force to figure things out for us. If I'm wrong about Dannik, then we can deal with the library when we find it. But if I'm right, and Dannik *is* killing people, then a dark-side curse may be the last thing we have to worry about."

After Zak left, Tash closed her eyes. She had just started to drift off, her mind relaxing, when . . .

Tash.

She opened her eyes. Had she heard someone whisper?

Tash.

She sat up. Someone had spoken her name. But her cabin was empty.

Tash.

For a moment, she felt like she was on the verge of sensing something, seeing something beyond the range of her eyes. It was like suddenly being plugged into a computer that could tap into all the information in the galaxy at once. Or maybe like becoming part of a starship's sensors, reaching out hundreds of light-years into the universe.

This strange sensation suddenly made Tash feel as if she

were slipping, falling away into the cosmos. Frightened, her mind slammed shut like a blast shield door. The voice in her head went silent.

Tash sat up and dressed quickly. Had she been dreaming? No, she was sure she hadn't fallen asleep yet. Heart pounding, she pulled on her clothes, put on her jacket, and slipped out of her room. Before she had shut off the message seeping into her brain, she had gotten a single, fleeing image of walls lined with ancient, dusty books.

The Jedi library.

Tash was tiptoeing through the solarium before she even thought about what she was doing. She didn't care if it had been a dream or not. She had something to prove to herself.

She remembered Deevee's words: Only a true Jedi could enter the library and resist the dark-side curse. Finally, she could test herself. She could stop wondering. She would know, once and for all, if she had the makings of a Jedi Knight.

She crept among the containers that marked the treasure hunters' small camps. She could hear them snoring or grumbling in their sleep as she made her way toward the sloping passageway. Moving quietly down the hall, Tash reached the deep ventilation pit. She had brought a small glow rod with her and lit it when she reached the end of the passageway. The light seemed small and weak hanging over the huge chasm.

Tash!

The voice reached her again, so strong and urgent that she nearly slipped over the edge of the pit.

Cautiously, Tash made her way down the narrow stairs until she reached the lower level. She passed over the spot where Mangol's body had been found and she shuddered. What had killed him? And was it waiting for her?

Despite her fear, Tash pressed on. She wanted to know, she *needed* to know, if she had the making of a Jedi Knight.

Her small glow rod bobbed like a tiny star as she went on into the darkness. As her light drove the darkness away, she found herself facing a wall at the far end of the passage. Just as she was about to turn back in disappointment, she spotted a row of six small, dark squares set into the metal wall. They looked like small maintenance tunnels, the kind humans or repair droids might use to crawl into the skeletal structure of the space station.

Had Mangol gone into one of these tunnels? Which one?

Tash stood before the six openings. One of them surely led to the Jedi library. The others could lead anywhere— she could reach a dead end, or get lost in an endless maze of interconnecting crawlways, or maybe slide down a chute into the depths of the abandoned station.

Tash took a deep breath. If she ever needed the Force, she needed it now.

As she stepped closer to the row of openings, a faint glimmer appeared before the fifth one from the left. A pale thin sliver of white, the opposite of a shadow, flickered in front of the opening, then vanished as quickly as it had appeared.

Tash!

The whisper rolled through her head again. But was it a voice leading her on or warning her to stay away? Tash went with her gut feeling.

She stepped through the fifth hatch and found herself in a long, low tunnel. She could feel her heart jump higher into her throat with each step. She was sure it was the right tunnel. She was sure that Mangol had come this way.

Fortunately, there were no more choices to make. The tunnel plunged straight through the heart of Nespis 8. At any moment, Tash expected it to open up into a fabulous chamber lined with thousands of ancient Jedi manuscripts.

Instead, the tunnel stopped.

A dead end. Tash thrust her glow rod forward to make sure she wasn't mistaken. The light showed her nothing but a cold gray metal wall.

"No, no, no," Tash muttered. She'd been wrong after all. She hadn't chosen the right tunnel.

In frustration, Tash slapped her hand against the dura-steel wall before her and turned back—only to hear a soft click and the whir of machinery behind her. Tash turned around.

The wall had vanished, sliding back into a hidden recess. She was looking at another stretch of tunnel. Twenty or thirty meters ahead, the darkness gave way to gray light.

She had found it.

Tash hurried forward, her fear replaced by excitement. At the end of this tunnel she blinked for a moment in a stream of white light that spilled in from a high-ceilinged chamber beyond.

She stepped into the light. As her eyes adjusted, she saw a large circular room. The walls were lined with hundreds of shelves, and on the shelves were rows and rows of ancient, dust-covered books. Two antique tables made of carved wood stood in the center of the room, with sturdy wooden chairs beside them.

I found it, she told herself. *I found it!*

In the midst of her own wonder, Tash heard the voice that had awakened her. But this time it did not whisper. It roared around her, loud, harsh, and full of rage.

GET OUT!

CHAPTER

Tash screamed.

She couldn't help herself. The angry voice came from all around her, striking her with the force of a punch in the stomach. But there was no one in the room. As the echoes of her scream faded down the long passageways, Tash was still looking around with wide, frightened eyes. She felt another wave of cold air wash over her, but this time a sensation entered her bones along with the chill. Fear.

Terrified, she backed away from the cursed room. But she was too slow. She felt the icy cold wave pass through her again. It was so strong that it overwhelmed her senses, and everything went black.

Tash woke to the feeling of a warm hand holding her own. Slowly, she opened her eyes, and blinked in the light of several portable glow panels. The bright light made a halo around Forceflow's gently smiling face.

"You'll be all right," he said softly. "Just relax."

She tried to speak, but fear seemed to have choked the words out of her. She knew she had to warn the others about the curse, but all she managed to rasp out was "Hoole."

"I sent for him," Forceflow said. "Your friends were in their ship. They'll be here any minute—"

"I'm here," said Hoole's sharp voice as the Shi'ido appeared next to Forceflow.

Like Mangol's cry earlier, Tash's voice had echoed up through the metal walls of the space station. Forceflow and the treasure hunters had come running when he'd heard her. Hoole was visibly relieved to see that his niece was safe.

"Tash, what are you doing down here?" he demanded.

Zak was right behind him. "Are you all right?"

Forceflow stopped all conversation. "By the Force! She found it!"

He pointed down the tunnel, where the entrance to the library was still visible.

"No, no!" Tash yelled, grabbing Forceflow's arm. "Don't go down there! It's cursed. It's haunted!"

Forceflow raised an eyebrow. "It's what?"

"There was a voice. There was no one there, but something shouted at me. But there was a . . ." She didn't know how to describe it. "It was like a wave of fear."

"Tash, calm down," said Forceflow, his blue eyes twin-

66

kling at her. "The most important thing right now is that you've done something no one else has been able to do. You've found the Jedi library!"

"Mangol found it," Tash muttered, "and he's dead."

Forceflow frowned. "True, but I'm sure that had nothing to do with the library itself."

"It did," she said dejectedly. "The legend says that only a true Jedi can break through the dark-side curse. The treasure hunter wasn't a Jedi, and"—she took a deep breath—"and neither am I."

Hoole put a gentle hand on Tash's shoulder.

Beside Hoole, Deevee said in the warmest voice his program could manage, "Tash, if that really is a Jedi library, then it would be the greatest galactic discovery in a hundred years."

Tash shook her head stubbornly. "I don't care. That place is dangerous. I'm not going back there."

Hoole's black eyes studied his niece for a moment, then the Shi'ido nodded. "Very well. We'll return to the *Shroud* to make sure you're all right. Then we can discuss our next step."

Forceflow disagreed. "You said yourselves that Gog is after you. In the library—with all the knowledge it contains—you might find a way to stop him. You're wasting valuable time."

The Shi'ido shrugged. "Our decision is made."

A dark cloud passed over Forceflow's handsome face but he said nothing. The others, however, were not so silent.

Domisari said she would return to the solarium as well, but the other two treasure hunters were reluctant to leave.

"We've been searching for the library for weeks," one of them said, "and we can't just walk away from it now."

Hoole returned to the solarium with Zak, Tash, and Deevee. Instead of entering the library himself, Forceflow followed them to the upper levels.

"Just think of it," Forceflow was saying as they reached the solarium. "Twenty thousand years of Jedi lore are stored in that one room. Think of the secrets those books must contain! All the mysteries of the universe may be answered there."

Hoole stopped short. "I hope you are right, Forceflow," he said. He pointed toward the pile of cargo containers that had marked the boundaries of Mangol's camp. "Because we now have another mystery to solve. Mangol's body is gone."

They all followed Hoole's long, bony finger. The Shi'ido was right. The body of the treasure hunter had disappeared.

Deevee asked the obvious question. "Who would have taken a corpse? And why?"

Looking around, Zak asked a question no one had considered. "Where is Dannik Jerriko?"

The others could not answer. They realized that Jerriko had not come when Tash screamed. And he wasn't here now. "I'm telling you, he's up to something," Zak insisted. "I'll bet he killed Mangol and now he's removed the evidence."

Tash was about to insist that there was no murderer, but before she opened her mouth, another cry drifted mournfully through the space station. It was followed by another, desperate, scream for help. The small group in the solarium looked at one another and every face grew pale.

They all knew what they would find at the library. The two treasure hunters were dead.

CHAPTER

Only a few people were left on Nespis 8 now. Aside from Hoole, Zak, Tash, and Deevee, Forceflow still remained, as well as the old woman Domisari, and the mysterious Dannik Jerriko.

The next day, after finally getting some sleep, everyone gathered outside the library.

No one believed Tash's story of an evil curse, but no one wanted to enter the chamber. Something was killing people, and none of them wanted to become the next victim. Only Deevee, because he was a droid, could enter. Tash and Zak hovered near the door as the droid entered the room and, careful not to touch them, examined the two bodies, which sat slumped at tables in the center of the library.

"There are no marks," the droid announced as he stepped away from the corpses.

"It's as though the life had been stolen right out of them," Forceflow mused. "Perhaps it *is* the work of the Anzati."

"It's the curse," Tash whispered.

Hoole frowned. "So far our only suggestions are a mythical species of killers and ancient dark-side magic. There must be a more logical explanation, and I know where to look for it."

The survivors formed a small circle in the solarium with Dannik Jerriko in the center. The narrow-faced man calmly studied his suspicious companions.

"This is ridiculous," Dannik was saying. "Do you truly think I have killed those pathetic fools? You might as well believe this girl's fear of a dark-side curse."

"We do not know what to believe," Hoole replied. "All we know is that three people are dead, and that you were missing when each of them died. And, again, when Mangol's body was stolen, you were the only one missing."

Dannik blinked very slowly. "This is a civilized Empire. There are laws, and this is not a court. You can't accuse me."

Hoole's voice was as cold as steel. "We are on the very edge of civilization. I have two young humans under my protection, and I intend to protect them by any means necessary."

Dannik locked eyes with Hoole. "Do not threaten me."

Hoole's gaze did not waver. "That is not a threat." Suddenly, the Shi'ido's entire body seemed to quiver. The skin seemed to crawl across his frame, and a moment later, Hoole had vanished. In his place stood a tall, shaggy Wookiee, who flexed and unflexed the claws of one massive hand. When the Wookiee spoke, its voice growled, but it still sounded like Hoole. "It is a promise," he said.

The fact that Hoole was a shapechanger made most people nervous. When he changed into something ferocious, most people quickly backed down. But Dannik seemed to become excited. His eyes flashed, and for a moment Tash thought he was going to attack Hoole. But then Dannik yawned and said, "Very well. You may threaten or promise or whatever you like, but the fact remains I did not kill those people."

"Then where were you when the murders took place?" Hoole growled, still in Wookiee form.

Dannik smiled coldly. "Come with me."

Hoole melted back into his own shape and Dannik led them to a small chamber just outside the solarium. At first Tash found nothing unusual about the square room, except for a strong smell of burning leaves. Then she noticed that one corner of the little room was covered with a thin layer of ashes.

Dannik produced a long, thin reed from his vest pocket—a pipe. "I confess that I have acquired a rather unpleasant habit. I smoke t'bac. Although I find the habit detestable myself, I have been unable to quit. In order to hide this personal failure, I prefer to smoke in private.'' He waited.

Zak squinted his eyes. ''Are you saying you were *smoking* during the murders?''

Dannik raised the pipe to his mouth and lit it with a small laser lighter. ''That is exactly what I'm saying.''

Deevee's photoreceptors glowed as they scanned the ash-covered floor. ''Master Hoole, there is a significant ash layer here. It would take quite a bit of smoking to produce this amount. I am inclined to say that this man is telling the truth.''

''But—'' Zak started to say.

''It seems,'' Hoole interrupted, ''that we owe you an apology.''

''Indeed,'' Dannik said stiffly. Without waiting for another word, he slipped past the others and returned to the solarium.

Zak and Tash watched Hoole and the others file out of the small room.

''But Tash,'' Zak said in a low voice, ''if Dannik's not the killer, then who is?''

''I think I know,'' replied a voice. It was Domisari. Her face was full of excitement. ''Meet me in fifteen minutes on the lower level, just outside the tunnel to the library. And don't tell anyone—not even your uncle!'' Then she slipped away.

''What was that all about?'' Zak groaned.

"I don't know, but I'm not sure we should go," Tash said. Her stomach had twisted into knots as soon as Domisari had spoken.

Her brother shrugged. "Have you got any better ideas?"

"Yes," she argued, "we could tell Uncle Hoole what she said, and tell him to come with us."

Zak scoffed. "Uncle Hoole would tell us we were being foolish."

With that, Zak headed for the passage to the lower levels.

"Zak!" Tash whispered after him. But her only answer was the hissing echo of her own voice.

She caught up to him at the edge of the huge ventilation shaft. Zak shivered. "I still don't get this coldness. If there were no power at all it would be even colder—like deep space. This is more like . . . a refrigeration unit."

"Or an air conditioner," Tash added. "This is a ventilation shaft, remember."

Zak shook his head. "Yeah, but there's not enough power in the space station to generate climate control."

"Can we worry about one thing at a time?" Tash snapped. "Come on, if we're going to do this, let's get it over with."

She did not like the idea of going near the library again. She was afraid of the curse, but even more than that, every step reminded her of the voice that had yelled at her to get out.

No one was waiting for them outside the tunnel to the library.

Zak looked to his sister. "Where do you suppose Domisari could be?"

"Maybe just late," Tash suggested hopefully.

Zak nodded halfheartedly.

They waited for five minutes, and then ten. The darkness seemed to crowd in around them. Once, Tash swore she thought she saw something floating just outside the circle of their light. It looked like fog. It was gone as soon as it appeared.

Finally her nerves got the better of her. "I can't stand just waiting here," she whispered. "Maybe Domisari meant that we should meet her *inside* one of the tunnels."

"That's not what she said," Zak argued.

"Well, she's not here. Besides, you're the one who wanted to come down here. So if we're going to talk with her, we should at least find her and get it over with. Come on."

Wanting to stay far away from the fifth tunnel that led to the library, Tash turned to the first passageway. "Maybe she's waiting down here."

The two Arrandas had traveled a few meters inside the tunnel when they heard the faint echo of footsteps behind them. They stopped and listened for a moment. Then a soft voice drifted through the darkness.

"Children . . . children . . ."

It was Domisari. They could see her approaching the tunnels. In one hand she held a glow rod. In her other hand gleamed an object made of black metal.

Tash was just about to call out to the old woman when a shadowy figure darted into Domisari's circle of light. The figure slammed into her with a jarring thud. The old woman grunted in surprise as she was shoved outside the circle of light and swallowed up by the surrounding darkness. Something clattered to the ground as sounds of a struggle reached them from the shadows.

"What happened?" Tash whispered as they stepped out of the tunnel. "Where are they?"

"There!" Zak said, pointing toward movement in the gloom.

Tash thrust the glow rod forward and gasped.

What she saw horrified her. A fallen blaster lay on the ground and over it, Dannik Jerriko and Domisari were locked in a struggle. Dannik was holding Domisari's head between his hands, and pressing his own face close to hers. There was a look of terror on Domisari's face.

And she saw something even more horrible.

Two small holes opened up in Dannik's cheeks. Out of each hole slithered a long, wriggling tendril. As Tash and Zak watched, the tendrils wormed their way across the short space that separated him from Domisari. They jabbed into her nostrils and crawled upward into her brain.

CHAPTER

Domisari was dead before her body hit the ground. Her lifeless corpse fell into a heap at Dannik Jerriko's feet as the killer turned to face the two Arrandas. They watched in horror as the two tendrils retracted. The tendrils were sucked back into the killer's cheeks and vanished, leaving no marks on his skin.

Tash swallowed. ''Zak, you were right.''

''No visible marks,'' Zak whispered, remembering Deevee's story about the Anzati. He looked at Dannik. ''You—You *are* an Anzati.''

''Wait,'' Dannik warned, ''it's not what you think . . .''

He took a step forward.

Zak and Tash turned and ran for their lives.

Blindly, they plunged into the first tunnel.

"Stop!" Dannik's voice called from behind. "Let me explain!"

They had seen Dannik kill Domisari in a matter of seconds without leaving a mark. They had looked into the eyes of one of the galaxy's most frightening species. That same creature now chased them down the tunnel.

An Anzati was after them.

"Y-You were right," Tash panted without slowing down.

"Remind me," her brother gasped as he ran in front of her, "to be wrong next time!"

Unlike the tunnel to the library, this one crisscrossed with a dozen other passageways. Zak and Tash could have used them to lose their pursuer, but they didn't want to get lost so they continued sprinting straight ahead. They had just begun to put distance between them and Dannik when they were pulled up short.

Another dead end.

"What do we do?" Zak said.

Tash could hear soft footfalls approaching them. She pictured the thin tendrils wriggling out from Dannik's cheeks, and shuddered.

"There was a secret door at the end of the other tunnel. Maybe there's one here too!"

She started pounding on the walls. Zak joined in, and together they banged at the metal walls with both fists.

But this time there was no secret door. The tunnel simply came to an abrupt halt. There was only a small metal grate set into the wall about waist high.

"Let's get the grate off!" Tash urged. The opening looked big enough for them to fit through.

The grating was as old as the rest of Nespis 8. When they both wrapped their fingers in it and pulled, the metal screen came off with a groan.

A putrid smell rose up from the hole in the wall. "Ugh! Smells like garbage!" Zak groaned.

"There's nowhere else to go!" Tash hissed. "Get in!"

Wrinkling his nose, Zak scrambled into the hole, and vanished.

The footsteps were closer. Tash followed her brother and wriggled her way into the opening. The vent traveled straight ahead for a meter, and then sloped sharply downward. Before Tash could stop herself, she was sliding down a metal chute, picking up speed as she went. She tried to brace herself against the walls of the chute, but they were too smooth. Suddenly she was launched into the air, then she splashed headfirst into a pool of thick, stinking slime.

Zak helped her up as she sputtered and coughed out a mouthful of stagnant water. They were standing knee-deep in a pool of liquid. Chunks of various objects—some hard like metal, some soft and squishy like old vegetables— floated around them. Tash took a breath and nearly gagged—the room smelled like something had been rotting there for centuries.

Tash listened. "I don't hear anything. I don't think he's followed us."

"Can't say I blame him. The smell down here could put

a bantha on its back.'' Zak waded toward the nearest wall. ''Let's find an exit and get back to the solarium. We need to warn Uncle Hoole about Dannik.''

Like everything else on Nespis, the garbage pit they had fallen into seemed immense. They splashed across the wide pool, wading around small hills of refuse as they used Tash's small, handheld glow rod to search for a way out.

As they struggled through the garbage-filled water, Tash began to feel uncomfortable—the way she felt when someone was staring at her. She looked around, but no one was there but Zak. Still, she could feel eyes boring into her.

Suddenly, Zak stopped. ''Watch where you're stepping,'' he said.

Tash blinked. ''What do you mean?''

''You just bumped your leg against mine,'' her brother said.

''No, I didn't.''

Zak paled. ''Well, *something* did.''

Uuuuhhhhhrrrrr.

The moan was low and distant, muffled by the pool of slime. They heard a distant splash, and then the *plunk* of something dipping back into the water.

Tash felt her heart bang against her ribs. ''We're not alone in here.''

She held up her hand so her small light would reach farther. ''There!'' Zak said, jabbing his finger.

Tash turned her head and caught a glimpse of a single

eye, resting on a thick stalk. The eye gleamed wetly as it studied them, then dropped quickly into the water.

"Dianoga," Tash breathed.

Dianogas were one-eyed, many-tentacled water creatures that lived in lakes and stagnant pools. Because they were scavengers, they could sometimes be found in the cesspools and sewer systems of planetside towns or large space stations, living off whatever was dumped into the garbage system.

Even if what was dumped was alive.

"Let's find an exit, fast!" Tash urged.

They quickly splashed across the wide pool. Ahead, they could see one wall of the large pit, and a small doorway half hidden by the gloom.

"There," Tash said, "we can get out th—"

Her next words were cut off as she was dragged down into the slimy water.

CHAPTER

At first Tash thought a piece of rope or cable had wrapped around her ankle. But as she was pulled under, she knew that the dianoga had her. One of its powerful tentacles had looped around her leg.

Tash managed to get her head above water, where she took in a lungful of air. Then she was dragged down again. Another tentacle slithered up her body and wrapped itself around her shoulder and neck, pinning her down.

The dianoga was trying to drown her in the shallow water.

Tash tore at the ropelike limb that held her, but the dianoga was far too strong. Her lungs started to burn.

"Tash, Tash!" Zak cried desperately. He had seen where she went down. He looked around desperately for a weapon and saw a long piece of durasteel pipe. It had been snapped in two, leaving a sharp, jagged edge. Snatching it up, Zak pressed the sharp edge against one of the dianoga's tentacles and began to saw at the tough, slimy flesh.

The single eye popped up from the surface a few meters from Zak to see what was attacking it. It stared at him coldly, studying its next meal. Then it plopped back below the water.

"Let's try that again," Zak growled.

He sawed at the tentacle some more and waited. "Come on, come on!" he urged. Tash couldn't hold out much longer. She was thrashing desperately.

Now Zak tried to pry the tentacle away. Again, the eye stalk shot up from beneath the water. This time, Zak was ready. Quick as lightspeed, he pulled the pipe free and swung with all his might. The metal tube smashed into the eye stalk, putting out its light.

A squeal rose up from somewhere beneath the slime. The tentacles suddenly flailed loose, splashing and flopping in the stagnant pool. Zak grabbed his sister by the jacket collar and hauled her to her feet. Tash came up gasping and sputtering for breath, her body and clothes soaked with the scummy fluid.

"Now's our chance!" Zak said, darting forward.

"Wait!" Tash blurted. She pulled him back. She had only been a few seconds away from drowning and she had no desire to be pulled under again. She remembered something Deevee had taught them. "Some water creatures are attracted by big movements, like splashes. We should try to go slow."

Zak agreed. Holding on to one another for support, they took slow, soft steps toward the door. They raised their feet gently out of the slime, and then softly put them back down, taking careful steps. It was nearly impossible, knowing that the dianoga was out there somewhere waiting to grab them. The urge to run was almost irresistible.

"This is driving me crazy," Zak muttered.

"Stay with it," Tash whispered. "I think it's working."

Uuuhhhhrrrrr. A low growl rose up from the water again. They heard the plink, plink of moving water and saw several tentacles wriggling about, searching for them. The single eye rose up above the water, but it blinked continuously and had filled with a bluish haze.

"That's one big black eye," Zak boasted. "I don't think it can see us."

"It can't find us," Tash said softly. "Just keep moving slowwwww . . ."

One of the tentacles swept toward them, but didn't reach far enough. Walking gently and patiently, Zak and Tash reached the door, a hatch set into the wall. They opened the hatch and quickly climbed out, then slammed the door behind them, locking the dianoga in the garbage pit.

"Are you all right?" Zak asked his sister.

Tash shuddered, and tried to wipe the slime from her

face and neck. "I think so. Just a little slimy. Thanks for saving me."

Zak grinned. "What are brothers for? C'mon, let's find a way out of here."

The passageway they were in was plain and unmarked, giving no hint as to where they might be. They knew they were deep inside Nespis now, well below the solarium and even farther down than the library level. Both Tash and Zak felt a cool draft flowing from their right.

"The ventilation shaft," Tash guessed. "It must be that way."

They hurried down the corridor. After a few minutes, they could see that it opened up into a wider room.

"Maybe that's the ventilation shaft," Zak said. "Then we can find the stairs and climb back up to the solarium."

The reached an opening, but it did not lead to the ventilation shaft. Instead, the corridor widened to a gallery like the one leading to the library.

But this one was full of bodies.

CHAPTER

The bodies were stored in rows inside large containers made of transparasteel and metal. Each container leaned against a wall and held one body. The tanks were surrounded by pipes and wires leading to a bank of computer equipment at the far end of the room. Inside each container, a cloud of mist covered the bodies like a fog.

Cautiously, they crept toward the closest of the tanks. Through its transparent walls, they could see the person inside. It was a human man—pale and lifeless. He wasn't breathing.

"Is . . . is he . . . ?" Zak started to ask.

"I think so," Tash answered. She shivered. "It's cold here."

Cautiously, Zak approached one of the containers and touched the transparasteel. He jerked his hand away.

"These containers are freezing. I think they're cryogenically sealed."

"Cryo what?" Tash asked. She was smart, but every once in a while her techno-loving brother came up with a word she didn't know.

"Cryogenically," he repeated. "It means the bodies are frozen so that they don't decay. Somebody is *preserving* these bodies for some reason." He exhaled and watched his breath appear in a thin fog. "This must be where the cold is coming from, not the ventilation shaft."

Tash took a few cautious steps toward one of the containers. "But what's this storage room doing in an abandoned space station? And who are these people?" she wondered. "Could this be left over from ancient times?"

Zak examined the wires and cables that ran toward the far end of the room. "I don't think so. This machinery looks brand new. Look at that."

Atop the computers at the far end of the room stood a large crystal globe. Inside, lights swirled and bobbed. The whole crystal glowed.

Zak said, "That thing doesn't look ancient. I'd say someone set up this equipment recently."

"And these people," Tash added. "The treasure hunters mentioned that people disappeared from Nespis 8 once in a while, but they thought the missing people either left or got lost. Maybe they're here! Someone's been *collecting* them."

"Dannik Jerriko," Zak guessed.

Tash shook her head. "No way. All the treasure hunters said he was a recent arrival. He couldn't have built all this equipment. But who did—and why?"

Zak looked at one of the bodies. "It reminds me of Necropolis." Zak had had a terrifying experience on the planet Necropolis—he'd been buried alive. He shuddered to remember it. "Well, at least we solved one mystery. We know that Dannik is the killer. You saw what he did to Domisari?"

Tash nodded, but she wasn't really paying attention. Something had distracted her, a faint whispering in her head, like someone talking from a great distance.

"I hope this convinces you that there's no dark-side curse," Zak continued. "Not that we're any better off, because I think Dannik is an Anzati, which means we're all in danger unless we can get to Uncle Hoole . . ."

Zak's words faded from Tash's ears. The whispering in her head had deepened and slowed to a murmur, the same whisper she had heard earlier. Only now it sounded more urgent. Another wave of cold fear washed over her. She steeled herself, trying to make sense of the voice. She took a deep breath to calm her tightening stomach, and focused on the voice.

. . . get out . . . get out . . . get out . . .

Tash concentrated. It was like trying to pick one voice out of a crowded room where everyone was talking. The voice grew clearer.

. . . get out . . . get out . . . get out . . .

It was the same voice Tash had heard in the library.

"Do you hear that?" she whispered to her brother.

Zak looked around. "Hear what?"

"That voice!"

"I don't hear anything." Zak noticed the tense look on his sister's face. "Tash? This place is as quiet as a lifeless moon."

Tash frowned. Why couldn't Zak hear it? The voice was all around them now, and it grew louder and stronger as she continued to focus.

GET OUT! GET OUT! GET OUT!

A voice can't hurt me, she told herself. *A voice can't hurt me.*

But what happened next hurt her a great deal.

There was no one near her, but Tash felt something brush against her neck. Just as she reached up to brush away whatever had touched her, two cold hands clamped down on her throat.

CHAPTER 13

Tash struggled against the hands wrapped around her neck, but the grip was unbreakable. She was being choked.

"Tash?" Zak said, as his sister clutched at her throat.

Zak! Help! Tash wanted to scream. Couldn't he see that someone was choking her? But she couldn't even breathe, let alone call for help.

With all her strength, Tash turned herself around.

No one was there.

The grip on her throat tightened.

Tash reached out desperately to her brother. As Zak stepped toward her, Tash felt the grip on her throat drive her backward. She was being pushed toward the wall.

"GETOUTGETOUTGETOUT!"

The voice roared in her ears. Tash braced herself to be crushed against the durasteel wall.

Instead, the moment she hit the wall it gave way, revealing a secret passage like the one that led to the library. *GETOUT! GETOUT! GETOUT!* Tash felt herself shoved hurriedly up the dark passage for twenty meters before she was suddenly dropped to the ground. The voice stopped.

Dizzy, Tash fought to get to her knees, and used the wall to brace herself as she tried to stand. She had reached her feet just as Zak came running up the tunnel.

"What was that?" he cried. "Are you all right?"

Tash shook her head. "No. None of us are. We're all in danger!" She told Zak about the voice that screamed in her ears, and the hands that gripped her throat.

"I didn't hear anything, Tash," her brother insisted. "And I'm telling you there's no curse. Dannik Jerriko killed those people."

"Then what grabbed me and pulled me twenty meters along this hallway?" she demanded.

Zak pointed back toward the morgue. "Maybe that place has an automatic defense system. It could have been a repulsor unit like the ones that power starships. Only this one was designed to push intruders out of the room."

"Come on, Zak—"

But Zak wouldn't let her argue. "Tash, we can talk about this later. Whatever happened, at least we found a way out of the morgue. We need to get back before Dannik kills anyone else!"

Tash agreed, and together they hurried along the tunnel, which curved upward.

Having gone down the stairs to the library level, and then sliding down farther to the garbage pit, Zak and Tash figured they were two levels below the solarium. They followed the passage upward for several hundred meters before it began to curve sharply to the right.

Zak set a fast pace. But Tash lagged behind, frightened. She could feel invisible eyes watching her from the dark— but it wasn't the same as when the dianoga had stalked them. Tash knew instinctively that these were not the eyes of a beast or a being. They were the eyes of whatever haunted the halls of Nespis 8. They were the eyes of whatever had grabbed her and thrown her out of that room.

"I think we've got a problem," Zak said.

Tash tore herself from her own thoughts. They had reached the end of the passage. Like the other passageways, this one ended at the ventilation shaft. But this time there was no stairway leading up or down—only a tiny ladder made of rails that had been welded into the side of the huge shaft.

Zak looked into the darkness above and below them. Then he pointed across the chasm. "I think that's the library across the way. That means we're only one level below the solarium, but on the wrong side. We could climb up, but I don't know how we'll get across."

"Okay," Tash said weakly. She wasn't afraid of heights and she didn't mind climbing. But she could still feel those powerful hands on her neck. If the spirit that haunted Nespis 8 decided to attack her while she was on that ladder, she knew that it was a long way to the bottom of the shaft.

Zak pulled himself out onto the ladder, and Tash slipped out behind him. Hand over hand they climbed up into the darkness. Tash's grip on the ladder rungs felt loose and slippery with her own nervous sweat. Halfway up the ladder, something tugged at her jacket and she shrieked, clutching at the rungs. But it was only a cold draft blowing up from the depths below.

Calm down, she told herself. *This isn't the way a Jedi would behave.*

But I'm not a Jedi, she thought. *If I were, I could have entered the library.*

After what felt like an eternity of climbing, they reached a small platform anchored to the solarium level.

"Keep your eyes and ears open," Zak warned. "Dannik could be around here anywhere."

Zak led the way down the passage. "It's hard to tell in the dark, but this hallway looks like it links up with the corridor between the docking bay and the solarium. Let's go."

His sense of direction proved true. Only a few dozen meters down the hallway, they reached an intersection. To the right, they could see the darkness give way to the gray light of the solarium. That meant the docking bay was in the opposite direction.

They turned left and hurried through the darkness until

they reached the huge docking bay. The pitch-black cavern was lit only by the running lights of the *Shroud*.

"Uncle Hoole! Deevee!" they called out before they had even reached the ship.

There was no answer.

Zak punched in the code that opened the ship's hatchway, and they scurried inside.

The ship was deserted.

Zak swallowed. "Maybe they're in the solarium."

The Arrandas hurried back to the transparent-domed room. But there was no one there either. They even found their way to Forceflow's private chamber, but he too had vanished.

Zak and Tash were both worried. Had Dannik gotten to everyone? Was he lying in wait for them?

"There's only one place left to check," Zak said quietly.

"We shouldn't go down there," Tash insisted. "I'm telling you, there's a curse."

"We *have* to look," her brother argued. "Uncle Hoole might be there." He waited for his sister to decide.

After a long pause, she finally nodded.

For Tash, every step toward the Jedi library was like trudging through fear. The air she breathed was heavy and thick, and her mouth was dry as the sands of Tatooine. But she forced herself to put one foot in front of the other until they reached the library. Just beyond the open doorway, they could hear someone moving around the room.

Zak's face brightened with relief and he rushed forward. "Uncle Hoole! Deevee, we—"

He stopped short. Hoole and Deevee were indeed in the library. But Deevee lay sprawled on the floor, deactivated, and Hoole sat slumped over a book, unmoving.

And over him stood Dannik Jerriko.

CHAPTER

"Murderer!" Zak cried.

Dannik Jerriko's face was unreadable. "That is true," he said. "I am indeed a killer. But I did not kill your uncle."

"Liar!" Zak replied with poison in his voice. "You've killed five people!"

A look of mild irritation crossed the killer's face. "I am an Anzati. In my lifetime I have killed many, many more people than that. But here, on Nespis 8, I have killed only one."

Zak had run into the room and knelt by Hoole. Tash looked on from the edge of the library. She wanted to run to Uncle Hoole but she still could not bring herself to step into the room. A barrier of solid fear blocked her path.

"So you are an Anzati," her brother said. "And you

followed us here from Jabba the Hutt's palace, didn't you?''

Dannik nodded. The tiny tendrils poked out of their hidden pockets in his cheeks, then retreated. ''I was there. I was hired to reach Nespis 8 before you.''

''Who hired you?'' Tash asked.

Dannik said nothing.

She tried again. ''Why did you kill Domisari?''

''I was hired to save you from another hired assassin,'' the Anzati replied.

Zak nearly choked. ''*Save* us?''

The Anzati pursed his lips. ''Apparently, someone high up in the Empire hired an assassin to track you down. I was hired to kill the assassin before she got to you. But I was unsure of her identity and had to wait. I got to her right before she shot you.''

Tash's head was spinning. ''You're saying that Domisari was a hired assassin, and that she was going to kill us?''

Dannik nodded. ''That was my assignment, and I have fulfilled it. I was just about to leave when I heard something down in the library. I found the Shi'ido and the droid here just before you arrived. There are no signs of life.''

As Tash cursed herself for her own fear, Zak put his hand on Hoole's wrist. ''It's cold,'' he whispered. ''He's not breathing.''

He knelt down next to Deevee and opened a small panel in the droid's chest. ''Deevee's not hurt—he's just been shut down!" Zak quickly adjusted a few switches in the droid's master control circuitry. There was a soft hum, and light suddenly flooded the photoreceptors in the droid's human-like face.

"Oh, oh, oh no!" Deevee cried. "Master Hoole!"

The droid scrambled to his feet and looked around, disoriented. "Zak, Tash, thank the Maker you're all right! Is Master Hoole—"

Tash could hardly bring herself to say the words. "I—I think he's dead. Deevee, what happened?"

The droid shook his metallic head. "I can't say exactly. When Master Hoole and I realized that you two were missing, we thought you might have come to the library. Once we were here, Master Hoole became intrigued by the books. He opened one . . . and . . . I remember sensing a powerful force that caused me to short circuit and . . . and . . . that's the last thing in my memory banks."

Zak frowned. "What about Dannik? Don't you have any memory of him?"

The droid looked at the murderer. "None whatsoever. I'm sure he wasn't here."

"It is as I said," the Anzati stated.

"This library is cursed," Tash said softly. "No one should have found it—ever. Now it's taken Uncle Hoole. We need to get out of here."

Dannik pursed his lips. "If you will excuse me, my own ship is waiting."

The Anzati strode to the door. Tash avoided his touch as

the killer slipped past her. "Wait!" Zak called. "Aren't you going to help us?"

The mysterious Anzati did not turn around as he sneered. "I am of the Anzati. We do not *help*." He vanished into the darkness.

The three companions stood frozen in place for a moment. Finally, Tash roused herself to speak. "What—What do we do?"

Deevee's caretaker programming kicked in. He knew that his priority was to make sure the Arrandas were safe. He said, "We must get Master Hoole's body back to the ship, and then leave here as soon as possible."

"What about Forceflow?" Tash wondered out loud. "Where has he been?"

"I have not seen him since we were all together. I fear that he, too, has fallen victim to this place."

Zak gently tried to lift Uncle Hoole's head from its place on the table. The Shi'ido's gray face sagged, pale and lifeless. He had fallen across one open book that he must have pulled from the shelves. Another book was clutched in his stiff, lifeless hand.

Zak accidentally brushed his hand across the book as he tried to lift Hoole, and it immediately turned to dust. The other book, still closed, was locked in Hoole's grip. Zak reached to pry it loose.

A warning cry shot through Tash's mind like an alarm bell. *No!*

"No!" she repeated aloud.

Too late. Zak pulled the book free. As he did, the leather-bound cover of the book opened. A blinding flash of light exploded like a supernova, turning the entire room white. Tash shielded her eyes.

When the light finally faded, Tash blinked away stars and tears from her eyes.

Zak lay in a crumpled, lifeless heap.

CHAPTER

"No!" Tash cried out again.

She forgot her fear. Her uncle and her brother, the last two members of her family, had just been struck down. She charged forward.

But as she did so, something melted out of the wall on the opposite side of the library. It was a ghostly figure, with almost no shape, just a ball of milky gray energy rolling through the air. As it floated toward her, two hands reached out of the center of the energy mass.

Tash yelled again. "Get away!"

"Tash?" Deevee knelt by Zak's lifeless body. The droid looked at her quizzically. "What is it?"

"Deevee, help! It's coming for me!" The ghostly image came nearer, the hands reaching once more for her throat.

"Tash, my sensors tell me that there's nothing alive in this room but the two of us."

"It's here! It's here!" She turned to run. "Deevee, come on!"

Confused, the droid did not move. He rechecked his sensors and found them in working order. He scanned the room again, pausing to search once more for even the slightest signs of life in Hoole and Zak.

Tash took a few frightened steps backward. The ghost had almost reached her—the hands were almost around her neck. Above them, where a face should have been, Tash saw a rolling blob of energy. A face seemed to be pushing its way out of the gray matter.

Sheer terror drove her backward. She couldn't wait for Deevee any longer, and turned back up the corridor. The ghost pursued, but at a slower pace. It seemed calm and certain that it would catch her.

In the light of her glow rod Tash saw that she had reached the false wall that hid the tunnel. Frantically, she searched for a control mechanism so she could shut the door and seal the ghost in. When she glanced down the hallway, the ghost still followed her. In the darkness of the hall it gave off an eerie glow.

"Come on, come on. There!" she muttered, finding a switch on the wall. She touched it, and the door slid back into place.

Tash backed farther up the tunnel, hoping she had sealed

the nightmare away. But a moment later the secret door shimmered, and the ghost melted through it.

Tash . . . Arranda.

The voice assaulted her from all sides.

"No! Stay away!" She turned and ran again.

In a flash she burst out of the tunnel. She found the stairs leading to the upper level and scrambled up to the solarium. She ran down the corridor until she reached the docking bay, then she hurried to the *Shroud* and raced onboard. She did not stop until her own door was sealed shut behind her.

She gasped for breath. Fear, sorrow, and anger welled up inside her. She was ashamed that she had abandoned Deevee and Zak, but the sight of the ghostly image had terrified her.

Tash had no idea how long she lay there. She kept hoping she would wake up and find that she was not on Nespis 8 and that Hoole and Zak were safe.

But she was already awake, and the only thing that came to her was an ominous sound.

Clunk. Clunk. Clunk.

Footsteps approached the *Shroud*.

"No," Tash whispered out loud.

Hrrrmmmm. The hatch opened. Footsteps started down the main corridor. They were headed for her cabin.

Did the ghost walk?

Tash could only stare wide-eyed as someone pressed a button and the door slid open.

Then she found herself staring into a pair of twinkling blue eyes.

"Forceflow!" Relief flooded through her. "How did you get in here?"

"I gave him entry," Deevee said, stepping into the door frame.

The dark-haired man smiled softly. "I found Deevee near the library. He said you had run away in a panic. We looked everywhere, then figured you'd come here."

"Where have you been?" Tash nearly sobbed. "Do you know what's happened?"

"I do," Forceflow said, grimly. "It's tragic."

"It's the curse," she said. "But it's not the library, it's the books themselves. When Zak opened one, there was a flash of light, and the next thing we knew . . ." She couldn't finish her sentence.

Forceflow sat down on the edge of her bed. "I'm beginning to think you're right, Tash. That old legend about the curse may be true. But that doesn't mean *no one* should enter the library."

She wiped a tear from her eye. "What do you mean?"

In response, Forceflow looked at Deevee. "What does the legend say exactly?"

Deevee replied, "That no one but a Jedi could enter the library unharmed."

"So what?" Tash said. "We don't have a Jedi."

Forceflow smiled. "We have you."

104

"Not funny," she sniffed. "I know I'm not a Jedi. I've never done anything but fail when I try to use the Force."

"I'm very serious." Forceflow stood up. "Tash, I've been researching the Jedi for years. I've made it my life's work. If there's one thing I'm sure of, it's that the Force is with you."

She shook her head. "No way. There's something in the library. Something real. It grabbed me. It almost killed me!" The news seemed to shock Forceflow. "Why would I want to go back there anyway?"

"Because the ancient Jedi knew many things," Forceflow said carefully. "They may even have known . . . how to bring back the dead."

Tash paused. "I've never heard of anything like that. I always thought the Jedi were one with the Force. They knew when it was their time to die. They wouldn't want to bring back the dead."

Forceflow shrugged. "Perhaps, perhaps not. Great secrets lie in wait down there. But we'll never know them unless you go down and break the spell."

Tash heaved a great sigh. The thought of those cold fingers around her neck still frightened her. But what did she have to lose? She had lost her parents months ago. She had lost her uncle. Now she had lost her brother, her only friend in the world. She had nothing left but desperate hope.

"Tash," Forceflow said, "Zak was a good boy. But he

didn't survive because he wasn't aware of the Force. You are. Don't you feel it?''

Tash didn't know what to say. Until recently, she had felt something. But now . . . "I don't know. There aren't any Jedi left to teach me. How do I know if I can use the Force?''

''Break the curse and open the books!'' Forceflow urged. ''All the answers are there!''

A few moments later Tash was walking down the corridor to the library. She had taken this way several times, but each time she had not wanted to go. This time, she forced herself forward. She was going into the library to face the curse of the dark side.

Her knees trembled.

Some Jedi, she thought.

The sound of Deevee's footsteps sounded reassuringly behind her. ''I still don't understand why Forceflow did not come with us,'' the droid said. ''There is safety in numbers.''

Tash whispered, ''Because he's not a Jedi. It wouldn't be safe for him.''

''It is not safe for *you*,'' the droid replied. ''I should not permit this.''

Tash half wished that Deevee *would* stop her from going. But without Hoole's commands, Deevee had only his own programming to go by, and he could find no alternative.

By the time she reached the entrance to the library, Tash was numb with sorrow and fear. But she was still aware enough to be stunned when she saw that the room was empty.

Deevee spoke the question she was asking herself. "Where have the bodies gone?" Zak and Hoole had disappeared, just like the treasure hunters. Their bodies had been whisked away to . . . where?

An image popped into Tash's mind. "The morgue," Tash breathed.

"Pardon?" the droid asked.

"Zak and I found a room filled with bodies. They were being preserved in freezing chambers. Maybe Zak and Uncle Hoole's bodies have been taken there."

Quickly, Tash described the entrance she and Zak had found: the ladder in the ventilation shaft, the sloping corridor, and the secret door. "That room has something to do with what's happening," she said. "Deevee, you have to go find them."

"I cannot leave you, Tash," the droid insisted.

Tash tried to sound braver than she felt. "Deevee, if anything's going to happen, you won't be able to stop it. Go find Uncle Hoole and Zak."

The droid hesitated. His computer brain, which could calculate a thousand probabilities in a nanosecond, could not solve this single dilemma. To stay with Tash although he would be of no use, or to find Zak and his master?

His brain reached a conclusion. Deevee turned and hurried away from the library.

Now Tash was alone. Truly alone. She had been dropped

as far down into a black hole as anyone could ever be. She was either going to be lost forever, or some miracle would pull her back into the light again.

She stepped into the library.

For the first time, she truly studied her surroundings. There must have been ten thousand books lining the high shelves, all of them ancient, and covered in layers of dust. She walked up to one shelf and began to read the words printed on the spines. Some were in alien languages, but most were in Basic, the common language of the galaxy. Some books were about science, others were about medicine, others about philosophy.

Tash stopped at one title that read *The History of the Jedi Knights.*

It seemed as good a place as any to start. Tash took the book down from the shelf without opening it. She took a deep breath. Amazed, she felt her fear melt away. She felt at peace. Tash didn't know what came after death, but she knew if there was anything, Zak would be waiting there for her. And her parents.

Tash started to open the book.

She never finished.

A powerful blow slapped the the book from her hand and sent it spinning against a wall. Surprised, Tash looked up to see what had struck her.

She found herself looking into the eyes of the ghost.

CHAPTER 16

Tash's knees were trembling so hard she almost fell to the ground. The ghost was no longer shapeless. It was still transparent and pale as death, but it stood before her in the form of a human man. Its cheeks were sunken. The tatters of its robe hung about it, faintly glowing, and there were gaping wounds in its body. If the ghost had been alive, Tash would have thought the wounds were marks left by a light saber.

"Tash Arranda."

The ghost spoke, not in her head this time, but directly to her in a voice so full of sadness Tash thought her heart would break if it did not stop from sheer fright.

"Wh-Who . . ." she tried to say.

"I have been trying to speak with you for some time," the ghost said in a low, moaning voice.

She backed toward the door. "Please . . . don't hurt me!"

The ghost drifted closer. "I am not here to hurt you, Tash. I'm trying to save you."

"Save me?" she asked. "But . . . you're the voice that kept threatening me. And you tried to choke me to death!"

The ghost spread its transparent arms in a helpless gesture. "I was trying to scare you out of the library, yes. But only because the library is dangerous. In the morgue, I managed to gather enough energy to push you toward the secret exit."

"Why didn't you just talk to me, the way you are now?" she said.

The ghost's face grew sadder. "I did not wish to hurt you, but I had to do something to save your life. When you were down in the morgue, you were in great danger, but you could not hear my voice. I had to do something to get you out of there." The ghost floated closer. "In all the years I have been here, no one has been able even to sense my presence. You were the first, but even you could barely see or hear me. I kept sending you warnings, but all you could do was *feel* them."

Tash's jaw dropped. "I kept feeling fear all around me."

"Those were my messages. You could not hear the words, but you sensed the danger. I have been with you since the moment you arrived on Nespis 8."

"Who are you?" she asked. "Are you . . . are you really dead?"

The ghost bowed its head in shame. "I was once a Jedi Knight. My name was Aidan Bok. I was in charge of guarding the old Jedi library, but I failed in my task. Years ago, Darth Vader came here to destroy the library. I tried to stop him, but he killed me and vaporized the library. Thousands of years of Jedi wisdom were destroyed, all because of my failure."

Tash said, "I thought that Jedi Knights passed on and became part of the Force when they died."

"I could not," the ghost said. "I was ashamed of my failure. I linger here, where I failed in my duty. This is my punishment, to remain here in this forgotten station." The ghost gestured to the terrible wounds in its body. "My body is gone, and I still bear the wounds Vader gave me. I don't deserve to return to rest in the Force."

She didn't know what to do or say. All she could think of was something her mother had always told her. "I'm . . . I'm sure you did your best. That's all anyone could ask."

The ghost suddenly lifted its head. Its eyes stared into the wall as if seeing something Tash could not. "You must go. There is great danger here."

Tash looked around. "Then this place really is cursed?"

"No. The dark-side curse is only a myth. Even the story that only a Jedi can enter is only a myth. This is not even the original library. That was destroyed long ago. Years later, an evil scientist came to Nespis 8 and built a new library. Then he started a rumor that the library contained powerful Jedi wisdom and he claimed that only those who understood the Force could safely enter."

"Why?" Tash asked.

"That lie was spread so people who think they have the Force would come to Nespis 8. This library is only a trap built by that scientist. I think he wants to capture the essence of a Jedi Knight. The devices in this library steal the life energy from anyone who opens a book here."

Tash thought her head would split from all the confusing information she was getting. "This doesn't make sense. Why would anyone go to all this trouble? There's no reason to fool people with fake books."

"Perhaps not normal people," the ghost replied in its hollow voice. "But someone sensitive to the Force might guess something was wrong and resist the life-stealer. The scientist needed to disguise his machinery. And it worked!" The ghost sighed. "For years I have watched victims come here looking for the old library, hoping to learn to become Jedi themselves. Instead, they have were captured by this trap. And I was helpless to save them."

"Why couldn't you warn them?" Tash asked.

The empty eyes stared at her. "Because I can only appear to someone else who has the Force."

Tash's mouth went dry. "But—But that means that I . . ."

"Yes, Tash Arranda," said the ghost. "The Force is with you."

Tash had longed to hear those words since the day she

heard of the Jedi. Now they rushed into her body like a bolt of energy. All her doubts were swept aside. She knew it. She had always known it. Sometimes, she realized, she just needed someone else to say it. She felt a warm electric tingle spread through her. It was familiar, and Tash recalled the other time she had experienced it. She had felt that same electricity on that day on D'vouran when she had met Luke Skywalker. Instinctively, she knew it was an awareness of the Force. The feeling took her breath away, and for a moment she could not speak.

It didn't matter. She had no chance to speak, because in the next moment Forceflow stormed into the library with an angry and impatient look on his face. He did not seem to notice Aidan.

"Tash!" Forceflow demanded. "Why haven't you opened a book yet?"

Tash didn't know where to start. Excited words poured out of her. "Forceflow! You won't believe it . . . I just learned that I'm . . . I mean, this library! We can't stay here! We've got to get out of here now. We're in danger. I just learned this from a ghost!"

Forceflow growled, "What are you babbling about, girl?"

Tash tried to calm herself. "This room is a trap. That's why people have been disappearing. I know it sounds strange, but I just learned this from a Jedi ghost. I can see him. He's right here in the room. I can communicate with him because I have the Force!"

Forceflow began to tremble with rage. His face twisted into a snarl.

"The Force! The Force!" he suddenly shouted angrily. "Blast the Force down the darkest black hole in the galaxy!"

And with that, Forceflow began to shiver. The skin crawled across his bones. Before Tash's eyes, Forceflow changed shape. His handsome face melted and morphed into the tall and terrible figure of Borborygmus Gog.

CHAPTER

Tash was stunned. The electric tingle, her awareness of the Force, vanished. "Not you. It can't be you!"

Gog loomed over her. Like Hoole, he was a Shi'ido and could change into any shape he chose. He had fooled her into thinking he was Forceflow. "Oh, but it is. This time, I will personally make sure that you never foil my plans again."

She took a step back. "Wh-What have you done with Forceflow?"

Gog threw his head back and howled with laughter. Still chuckling, he turned his evil glare on Tash. "Stupid child. I *am* Forceflow. I have *always* been Forceflow!"

Tash was stunned. It was impossible. "That's not true!" she replied. "Forceflow works against the Empire. He keeps the legends of the Jedi Knights alive. He's a hero!"

"Yes. And he also exists only in *your* head." Gog laughed evilly. "Forceflow is a trap, just like this place. I wanted to capture people with the Force. I knew the Emperor had killed all the Jedi. I had to find someone who did not know the Force was with them. So I created Forceflow to attract people interested in the Jedi Knights. Just like you."

Tash felt like her heart had suddenly frozen. "You made me think Forceflow was a hero. You made me befriend . . . *you.*"

Gog chuckled. "Yes, I did."

Tash felt her frozen heart break into pieces.

Gog laughed. "Don't feel bad. You weren't the only one. I did the same to dozens of people. Once I made contact with them through the HoloNet, I lured them to Nespis 8 where I could trap them with this library."

"Why?" Tash could not help but ask.

Gog grinned. "Because I knew that sooner or later, I'd find a victim sensitive to the Force." Gog nearly spat when he said the words *the Force*. "The Force is the final segment of my project."

He held out his grasping fingers as if to grab Tash. "I have waited. *Patiently.* For years! My library has trapped the life energy of hundreds of people, but not a single one of them was useful."

Tash's mind reeled. "You've been killing innocent people."

"Stupid, stupid human," Gog spat. "I wouldn't go to so

much trouble just to kill them. They're in stasis. I can use them even if they don't have the Force. I've been studying their life essence, trying to understand what makes things *live*."

"You captured their life essence?" she asked. "You mean, those bodies are still alive?"

"In a manner of speaking. But I have no intention of returning their essence to their bodies. Certainly not that meddling Hoole. I'll enjoy knowing that Hoole's very essence is trapped within my machinery." Gog's eyes gleamed coldly. "I've wanted to get revenge on Hoole for twenty years."

Twenty years? Tash and Zak had been with Hoole when he discovered Gog's first experiment, the living planet. But that had only been a few months ago.

Tash recalled Hoole's mysterious past. Obviously, Gog and Hoole went back much farther than Project Starscream.

Gog saw the confused look on her face and grinned. "Oh, yes, you were right about one thing, Tash. Your uncle Hoole has a dark past. A *very* dark past."

"I don't understand—" she started to say.

"You don't need to," Gog interrupted. "I have waited long enough to find a Force user. Now I have one."

Gog suddenly raised a blaster. He pointed it at Tash. "Now, Tash. Open the book."

Tash held the book in her trembling hands. It looked innocent enough—an old volume with a leather cover. Gold
letters were stamped across the front.

But it was a trap. The minute she opened it, Gog's machines would suck the life force from her body, trapping it
forever. She was too frightened to move.

"Tash."

The voice of Aidan snapped her from her trance. She had
been so overwhelmed by the appearance of Gog that she
had forgotten the Jedi ghost.

She looked for him now. The gray figure was still hover-
ing next to her, gazing at her with his empty eyes.

"Aidan, help me," she pleaded.

"Stop mumbling and open the book!" Gog pointed his

blaster at her head. He obviously could not see or hear Aidan.

"I cannot help you," Aidan sighed. "I lost my power long ago, when I failed to defeat Vader. I am no longer a Jedi."

"But you were able to touch me. You shoved me through a doorway!" Tash cried.

Gog raised an eyebrow. He followed Tash's gaze, but all he saw was empty air. "I will give you to the count of three," the evil Shi'ido threatened. "If you do not open the book, I'll blast you to atoms. I promise you, the Essence Stealer is far less painful."

Aidan frowned at Tash. "I was able to touch you because we are connected by the Force. I drew on your link with the Force to become more solid, just as I draw on it now to become visible to you. But that's all I can do. I tried to be a hero once, Tash, and I failed."

Tash realized that Aidan sounded just like her. She had thought one failure meant the end of all her hopes. She had sulked. She had given up her dreams of becoming a Jedi until Aidan told her that she had the Force. She had just needed someone to tell her what she already knew in her heart.

Maybe that's what Aidan needed too.

Gog heard none of this. He began to count. "One."

"Aidan!" she begged. "You're only a failure if you think you are."

The ghost whispered, "I wish I could believe that, Tash. But the Force is no longer with me."

"But you said we were connected by the Force! That means we both have to have it! Please!"

"Pretending to be insane won't help you," Gog said. "Open the book. Two!" His finger tightened on the trigger.

"But I'm too weak," the ghost said.

"Try!" she begged. "If we're connected, maybe we can do it together."

There was flicker of light in the ghost's eyes. "I'll try. Tash, focus on the blaster. Use the Force to pull it from his hand."

Tash turned to Gog. As she did, time seemed to slow down. She saw the black weapon gleam in Gog's hand. She felt her connection to the Force. Focusing all her willpower, she imagined the Force reaching out. Beside her, she knew that Aidan was doing the same.

For a second, just a brief instant in time, she felt something surge out of her.

"Three," Gog said. He fired.

Tash's Force-power was too weak to pull the blaster from Gog's grip. But something made his hand jerk downward and his shot went awry. The blaster bolt shattered the floor at his feet and sent up a shower of sparks. For a moment, the Shi'ido was lost in a cloud of smoke.

"Run!" Aidan urged.

Dropping the book, Tash slipped past Gog and raced up

the hallway. The Jedi ghost was right beside her, gliding smoothly along the floor.

"He is coming," Aidan warned.

Tash could already hear Gog's footsteps pounding after her.

"I've got to get to the morgue," she said. "Zak and Uncle Hoole are still alive!"

Aidan tried to help. "The fastest way is to go down the ventilation shaft and—"

"I'm not going to go that way," Tash interrupted. Maybe it was the Force, or maybe it was just hope, but a clear plan suddenly formed in her mind. "I've got a better idea."

Reaching the end of the hallway, Tash found herself in the gallery where they had discovered Mangol's body. She turned around to face the six maintenance tunnels. She'd just come out of the fifth one. Now she plunged into the first.

"Running is useless!" Gog roared behind her. "There is no place to hide from me!"

It was a long way to the end of the tunnel, but Tash refused to slow down. She would not give up. She reached the end of the corridor and found the garbage chute she and Zak had used before. She dove in.

The ride was as slick and smooth as before, and she smelled the stench of garbage before she flew out into the pit and dropped into the slimy pool. The loud splash she made caught the attention of the room's occupant.

Uuuhhhhhrrrrrr.

Aidan melted through the walls. "Tash, have you forgotten? The dianoga is here!"

"I know," she replied, wading toward the exit door.

She heard Gog's voice echo down the garbage chute, and she knew that he was following her down.

Tash forced herself to slow down, taking small steps, making as little splash as possible. She knew the dianoga could not see well. It would have to rely on splashes in the water.

But I'm not going to make any, she thought.

Gog could not say the same. The Shi'ido plunged feet first into the cesspool, landing ten meters away with a loud splash. He held up a glow rod, and Tash saw his angry face. "I told you you could not hide from me!" he growled.

"You haven't caught me yet," she retorted.

Roaring, Gog charged forward, splashing his way toward her. But before he'd covered half the distance, the Shi'ido stumbled and gasped.

A thick tentacle had wrapped itself around his waist. "No!" Gog yelled. Then he was pulled under the surface of the slimy pool.

Tash didn't wait to celebrate her victory. She hurried to the exit hatch and dragged her sopping body out of the garbage pit.

Following the cold air, Tash found herself once more in the morgue. She shivered—and not just from the cold. She knew that the bodies in the containers were still alive, their life force trapped in Gog's machinery. Tash saw that there were two new containers in the room. She rubbed frost away from the transparent covering . . . and saw her brother's face. In the next container lay Uncle Hoole.

"Tash!" a familiar voice called. Deevee stepped from behind one of the two containers.

Tash was delighted. She had almost forgotten that she'd sent Deevee down to the morgue. The droid pointed to the two containers. "I have spent several minutes examining this equipment. If I'm not mistaken, there is some possibility that these victims are still alive—"

"They are!" Tash said. "Their life essences are trapped in that crystal globe. We have to reverse the process."

Deevee's mechanical shoulders slumped. "As you know, my computer brain is quite powerful, but I'm afraid this technology is too complex, and that knowledge is beyond me. I don't know how."

"I do."

Tash looked at Aidan. The flicker she had seen in the ghost's eyes had grown to a steady light. "You do?" she asked.

"I've spent years watching Gog set up his experiments here and trap people. I was helpless to stop him, but I know how his equipment works."

"Lead the way," she replied.

"Tash, to whom are you speaking?" Deevee asked.

Tash smiled. "I'll tell you later."

Aidan guided them to the computer panels beneath the

crystal globe. Tash watched the glowing, swirling mass inside. Somewhere, trapped in that globe, were Zak and Uncle Hoole.

Aidan quickly guided Tash through a series of controls. When she was done, he pointed to a large red lever. "There. Just activate this energy transformer. It should cause feedback through the life-stealing device and reverse the process. The life forces within the crystal should return to the proper bodies in the containers."

As Tash reached for the lever, a blaster bolt struck the ground beside her. She jumped back, startled.

"Get away from the lever!" said a commanding voice.

Tash and Deevee spun around.

There stood Gog. His clothes were half torn, and a terrible scar ran down the side of his face. But he was still holding the blaster in his hand.

CHAPTER

Gog's body trembled with anger. He looked exhausted from his fight with the dianoga, and he leaned against one of the tanks for support. But the blaster was steady in his hand. "The Essence Stealer would have been unpleasant, but not too painful," he said in a voice as sharp as a vibroblade. "But a blaster set on heavy stun will leave you sick for days. Of course, by the time you come around, I'll have picked your Force-sensitive brain clean."

Gog fired his blaster.

Tash winced, but the bolt never struck her. It was intercepted in mid-flight by Deevee. The energy bolt shattered his chest plate and sent him clattering to the floor in a shower of wires and sparks. For a moment, both Tash and Gog stared down in surprise at the heroic droid.

Then Tash dove for the lever.

She pulled it before Gog could fire again.

The results were immediate. Energy seemed to stream from the crystal globe, crackling and sparking along the pipes, flashing toward the containers. Circuits began to pop, and smoke began to rise from every container touched by the energy surge. In seconds, all of them were aglow.

"No!" Gog shouted.

He raised his blaster to fire again just as the power surge reached the container where he stood. A fountain of sparks burst from the container's circuits, bathing Gog in a shower of electricity. The force of the small explosion hurled the Shi'ido backward, his clothes smoldering. The blaster flew from his hand and clattered to the ground a few meters away. It had melted into a lump of metal.

Gog struggled to his knees. The hand that had held the blaster was blackened from the explosion, and other burns streaked his face and body. The evil Shi'ido swore a curse in a language Tash didn't know, and he ran.

"We can't let him get away!" Tash said.

"He's heading for the secret passage," Aidan replied.

Tash looked around. There was no one to help her. Zak and Hoole were stirring, but in no condition to walk, much less run after Gog. Deevee looked terribly damaged. She saw a glow rod lying near one of the freezing chambers and snatched it up.

"Come on," she said.

She started after Gog, with the Jedi ghost drifting beside her.

Hurrying up the secret passageway, Tash heard the clanging echo of her boots on the metal flooring. But even louder than her own movements, she heard the struggling gasps and wheezes of Gog as he tried to escape. She could tell he was badly wounded, and every step caused him pain.

She gained steadily, and soon she could see him laboring at the edge of her light. He was a crazy sight. Every five or ten steps, the Shi'ido tried to change shape. One moment she was chasing after a lizard-like tauntaun, the next she was after a scrambling runyip, and the next she was chasing a shambling nerf. But each shape-change seemed to cause the wounded scientist terrible agony, and finally with a cry he shifted back into his own form.

She reached the end of the passage and the huge ventilation shaft. The light from her glow rod revealed the scientist's twisted face. Beyond him hung the open air and darkness of the wide pit. At the edge of the pit was the ladder Zak and Tash had climbed earlier.

"Gog!" she yelled.

The Shi'ido turned. "Vader was right. I should have killed you when I had the chance. But that time will come, I swear it!"

Gog turned to grab the ladder.

"Don't!" Tash called. "You're too badly hurt. You'll never make it!"

Gog ignored her. His blackened hands clutched the rails, and for a moment, Tash thought he would get away. But as he started to climb, his wounded hands failed him. He started to slip. Tash lunged forward, but she was too late.

Gog flashed past her as he fell. In a desperate attempt to save himself, the Shi'ido was shapeshifting into every form he could think of. But nothing could save him. With a wordless cry, Gog fell away from the ladder and Tash watched his gray form shrink into the void.

"No one's ever found the bottom," she said, remembering the words of the man she thought was Forceflow.

Aidan peered down the great shaft. "There is a bottom," he said, "but it's a long, long way down."

Tash and Aidan hurried back to the morgue. As they arrived, the occupants of the freezing chambers had begun to stir. Those who had been trapped the shortest time—the treasure hunters, Zak, and Uncle Hoole—rose first, staggering out of their containers and looking around in amazement.

Tash dropped the blaster and ran to her brother, who was running his hands through his tousled hair like someone who had awakened with a headache.

"Zak, you're alive!" Tash yelled.

"Are you sure?" he groaned. "I don't feel like it."

Hoole looked around, taking in the machinery, the crystal globe, and Tash all at once. "You must tell us what happened, Tash," Hoole said, "but please begin by explaining what has happened to my droid."

"Deevee! He saved my life," Tash started. She ran and

knelt at his side. "Deevee, are you all right? Can you function?"

Live wires still sparked and burned around Deevees' chest plate. He looked heavily damaged. "I will need replacement parts," he said. He stared sadly at the hole in his chest plate and heaved an electronic sigh. "One would think that, with a brain as powerful as mine, I would have come up with a better plan."

"You saved my life, Deevee," Tash said, wrapping her arms around the metallic hero's shoulders. "Thanks."

As quickly and clearly as she could, Tash told them what had happened.

Hoole listened intently. "Are you sure Gog is gone?"

"I saw him fall. No one could have survived that."

Hoole nodded, then pointed to the many people struggling to crawl out of their freezing chambers. They looked dazed and confused. "Zak, Tash, help free these people. I need to examine this equipment." Without waiting for their answer, Hoole turned and began to study the equipment Gog had left behind. A look of deep concern settled over his face.

Zak and Tash did as they were told, quickly pulling Gog's victims from their small prisons and assuring them they were all right now. Tash helped Mangol crawl from his chamber and plop down on the floor, rubbing his temples.

"You're all right," she assured him. "Everything's going to be okay."

The fortune-seeker barely heard her. He was delirious, and kept mumbling, "I found it though. The library. I found it, it's all mine. Heh, heh. All mine."

Tash shook her head and muttered to herself, "You're welcome to it," before moving on to help someone else.

Tash and Zak had just gathered the prisoners together, and done their best to explain what had happened, when Hoole turned away from the Essence Stealer. "This equipment is very technical. I'm not sure I understand all of it. But if I'm right, Gog was trying to manipulate the Force."

Tash looked at Aidan, who nodded. "That's right," she said.

Hoole shook his head, and Tash heard him mutter, "He has been tampering with power that could destroy the galaxy itself. This time he has gone too far."

"Well, at least he's been stopped, once and for all," she said.

Hoole raised an eyebrow. He seemed surprised that she'd heard him. "Perhaps," he said. "Perhaps."

EPILOGUE

Tash, Zak, and Hoole helped Gog's prisoners back to the docking bay. There were several ships left on Nespis 8. At least one of them, they guessed, had belonged to Domisari. Another belonged to Mangol. As soon as Hoole was sure that the ships and the rescued prisoners were fit to fly, he turned his attention away from them and back to his own ship.

"They can all get off Nespis 8. Now it's time we did. And fast."

Hoole and Zak carried Deevee onboard the *Shroud*. Tash stayed behind a moment longer.

She hadn't told anyone about Aidan. There hadn't been time. And, she thought, it might be too difficult to explain.

The ghost seemed to read her mind. "It will always be difficult, Tash. There will always be those who do not *want* to understand the Force. But you'll be fine." He smiled.

Now that Tash had a chance to catch her breath, she noticed that the Jedi ghost had changed. His face no longer looked haunted, and his cheeks had fleshed out. He now looked completely distinct—hardly like a ghost at all, except that a faint glowing light surrounded his body.

"Your wounds are gone," Tash noticed.

The ghost nodded. "Thanks to you. Soon I'll leave this place, to join with those Jedi who have passed into the Force. You helped me remember that the Force is always

131

with me. Wounds—all wounds—eventually heal. Only the Force lasts forever."

"The Force," she whispered. "I can't believe it's real. I mean, I can't believe it's with me. What do I do?"

"Follow your heart. Seek help from those around you," Aidan replied. In the dim light of the docking bay, he seemed to fade.

"Like who?" Tash asked. "My brother? He's only just now starting to think the Force is real."

Aidan smiled again. "He may surprise you. Goodbye, Tash."

"Wait!" she called out. "I have a million questions. What do you mean about Zak?"

But the ghost of the Jedi was gone.

Tash lingered inside Nespis 8 a moment longer. She would never forget that in those dark, haunted hallways, she had finally touched the Force. She turned and hurried into the ship.

Long after the echoes of the *Shroud*'s engines had faded from Nespis 8, the scream of Imperial TIE fighters made its walls shiver. The rumble of Star Destroyers nearly shook its foundations to shards. A battalion of stormtroopers swarmed over the abandoned space station. Once it was secure, a single shuttle cruised ominously on board, and a black-armored figure stepped out.

Darth Vader stopped. He reached out with the dark side of the Force, scanning the station. In an instant, he knew they had come too late. His assassin, Domisari, was dead.

Hoole and his companions were no longer there. Gog was nowhere to be found—Vader was sure he was dead. His dark mind swept over the morgue, where Gog's machinery still smoldered. Instantly, the Dark Lord knew what Gog had been trying to do.

"Fool," the man in the mask told himself. "There is only one way to master the Force, and that is through the dark side."

Vader was about to turn back into the ship when he paused. He felt something . . . a disturbance in the Force. It was tiny, almost insignificant. But it was there, like a footprint left in the sand.

Another Jedi?

No, Vader told himself. He had destroyed all the Jedi. He had even killed one here, on Nespis 8, years ago. That's what he must have felt. The echoes of that long-ago battle.

He turned to a waiting stormtrooper. "Recall your men, commander. Nespis 8 is dead."

With a swirl of his cape, the Dark Lord returned to his ship and departed.

Had he lingered a moment longer, Vader might have detected something deep in the bowels of the space station. At the bottom of a deep ventilation shaft, in darkness as profound as a black hole, a figure stirred. The fingers of a burned and blackened hand twitched, and a dark eye opened . . .

Hoole, Tash, and Zak continue their journeys to the darkest reaches of the galaxy in *Army of Terror*, the next book in the Star Wars: Galaxy of Fear series. For a sneak preview, turn the page!

Tash stopped listening. A motion caught her eye. It was small—but on a planet with absolutely no life, she noticed it right away. She thought she'd seen something step from behind one of the rocks. But when she turned to get a better look, all she saw was the rock's own shadow. She shrugged.

". . . and according to the articles I've read," Deevee went on, "the Kivans may have left behind entire cities in the aftermath of Mammon's disaster . . ."

"I believe that is enough background, Deevee," Hoole said shortly.

"But Master Hoole, surely you appreciate how interesting this planet must be to an anthropologist! It's a dead civilization."

"I know. I *am* an anthropologist," Hoole said. But he said nothing more.

A moment later something caught Tash's eye again. But when she turned again to look, there was nothing but shadows. For a moment, she thought she could see the shadows stretching toward them. But then she realized it was only the setting sun, making the shadows grow longer on the ground. Still, something had caught her eye . . .

"Uncle Hoole," she asked, "is it possible that there's still something alive here?"

"No," Hoole said definitely. "Every living thing on Kiva died."

"But I thought I saw something—"

"A trick of the light," the Shi'ido interrupted.

"But something fired at us," Zak said. "There's got to be someone here."

"Not someone. Something," Hoole said as they came to the top of a small hill. "Look."

On the other side of the hill, nestled in a small, barren valley, stood a large tower. An ion cannon was mounted atop the tower, its tip pointing up into the gray sky. The tower hummed with energy as it swiveled automatically on its base.

They walked down into the valley. Here, the shadows were even thicker.

"It is a computerized defense system," Hoole explained. "It's fully automated."

"How did you know that?" Tash asked.

Hoole shrugged. "The sensors picked it up just before we were hit." The Shi'ido looked at his niece and nephew. "So, as you can see, we are quite alone on this planet."

Uncle Hoole always has an explanation for everything, thought Tash, as she wandered away from him and Zak. She picked her way through the maze of toothlike rocks toward the ion tower. *It's so much darker here in the valley*—Tash couldn't believe how fast the shadows moved here. As Zak and Hoole's voices faded in the distance, Tash stood still, looking all around her, trying to see just how the rocks cast such weird, fast-moving shadows.

Suddenly, Tash screamed. Something had grabbed her by both wrists—she was being attacked!

ABOUT THE AUTHOR

John Whitman has written several interactive adventures for *Where in the World Is Carmen Sandiego?*, as well as many Star Wars stories for audio and print. He is an Executive Editor for Time Warner AudioBooks, and lives in Los Angeles.